Death on the Rocks

Lily Larkin Mysteries
Book 1

Hannah Ellis

Published by Hannah Ellis
www.authorhannahellis.com
Postfach 900309, 81503 München
Germany

Cover design by dmeacham design

Death on the Rocks

Chapter One

SATURDAY

THERE WAS A SMALL, but undeniable chance that Lily Larkin was going crazy. For the last six months she'd been on a mission to track down an ice cream shop.

An ice cream shop, for goodness' sake.

Not just any old ice cream shop, of course. A specific one. The last time she'd visited it she'd been a small child so she didn't know its exact location. According to the back of the photograph it was in Cornwall. And while Cornwall wasn't a particularly large county, it was still an extensive search area for one person to cover – with a lot of ice cream shops. She'd flashed that photo around every town and village in the county as though she were searching for a missing person.

Finally, she'd got a promising lead. The fisherman she'd spoken to in Torquay swore he'd been to the shop as a child too and provided her with its exact location. It was just Lily's luck that the shop was in the remotest part of Cornwall. The island of St. Mary's was stuck all the way out in the Atlantic – twenty-four miles off the UK's southwest coast.

So that's where she currently was. With any luck, today would be the day she'd return to the place which held her only memories of her parents.

A loud crash made her set aside the photograph she'd been staring at and move to the window of her room in the cosy bed and breakfast.

It hadn't been Lily's first choice of accommodation. Hotels were more her vibe. Somewhere big and impersonal where she could go unnoticed. Given her last-minute plans, she hadn't had much choice, especially given the limited accommodation options on the Isles of Scilly.

At least the accommodation was on St. Mary's – the largest of the five inhabited islands in the archipelago. The B&B had been the only accommodation with availability. It boasted a mere three bedrooms and a shared bathroom. Definitely not ideal, but the owners, Mr and Mrs Miller, had been very welcoming when she'd arrived the previous evening. The friendly couple lived in the converted garage at the side of the house with direct access to the house via the kitchen, off the breakfast room, where Lily had just eaten.

During a disappointingly mediocre breakfast, Mrs Miller had eagerly introduced Lily to the other guests, which really left her longing for the anonymity of a hotel chain.

Being dragged into the breakfast room conversation did, however, mean that Lily knew what was currently going on outside, making the sight of people moving furniture from the living room out into the garden less perplexing than it would otherwise be.

The striking blonde woman in the centre of the garden was some kind of social media influencer. At breakfast, she'd seemed a little offended that Lily hadn't heard of her, and had handed over her business card with a dismissive flick of her hand.

Lily pulled it from her pocket now and went into her phone. The first image which came up when she searched for Alanna Harding showed her tall, toned body draped across an imposing leather wingback armchair in the middle of a deserted white sand beach. It gave a little more context to the living room furniture in the garden.

A website link took Lily to a travel and lifestyle blog which she had zero interest in. Apparently these days it was possible to make a living pouting on random furniture in exotic places. The text that accompanied the pictures was neither insightful nor grammatically correct, but it seemed Alanna's followers were happy to overlook those details. The comment section was filled with questions about the shade of her lip gloss and where to buy the boots she was wearing.

Returning her gaze to the bustle in the garden, Lily watched Alanna's boyfriend, Marc, sidle over and slip his arms around her waist before almost immediately being given the brush off and directed to reposition furniture.

Mr Miller – a tall, wiry man – carried a cumbersome coffee table outside with a young guy who apparently helped around the house and with some gardening. Oscar looked to be in his late teens and appeared thoroughly unimpressed with the current situation.

At the side of the garden, leaning on a wall and inhaling deeply on a cigarette was the photographer for Alanna's blog. Vinny had looked Lily up and down when they'd been introduced, making her feel exposed. If she was feeling generous she might have thought it was his artistic eye that had him looking at her so intensely, but it didn't feel like that.

Now, he looked bored as Alanna called out to him and beckoned him over. Stubbing out his cigarette, he retrieved his bulky camera from its perch on the wall and ambled over to her.

With a small shake of her head, Lily moved away from the window and plucked the photograph from the bed, to stare once again at the faces of her parents, smiling happily into the camera alongside a younger version of herself. Not for the first time, she went into her phone to check her route from the bed and breakfast to the promenade by Porthcressa Beach.

From there, she shouldn't have a problem finding the ice cream shop. Or at least the building it used to reside in. There was no mention online of it still being an ice cream shop, but the location also didn't bring up anything else in any of her searches so there was a chance it was still there with no online presence.

What she'd do when she found the place wasn't clear to her yet, but she'd figure that out later. She told herself it wasn't nerves that made her move slowly. The long shower she took wasn't a way to put off concluding the search for the ice cream shop. Nor was the slow pace at which she packed her backpack and put on her hiking boots. There was no rush, that was all. No reason to hurry.

Finally, she pulled a faded grey hoodie over her plain V neck T-shirt and headed for the door with her backpack slung over one shoulder.

Halfway down the stairs, she paused at the sound of hushed voices drifting from the breakfast room. Lily's ears pricked up and she stayed absolutely still.

"She has a huge social media following," Rodney Miller hissed at his wife. "One of these influencers. If she writes a bad review, it'll be the end of us."

"Don't be so dramatic," his wife, Flora, replied. "One critical review wouldn't be the end of the world. Especially if she rates us badly on something as stupid as whether we let her move every piece of furniture we own to the garden." She huffed out a breathy sigh. "I can't believe you agreed to this nonsense. And then carted it all out there for her. If your back starts playing up you'll get no sympathy from me."

"My back is fine. And you're underestimating the power of

reviews. We've had a spate of less than stellar ones recently. I'll bet that's why we've been getting cancellations."

"It was only a few cancellations," Flora said flatly. "And maybe the bad reviews are a sign that we should think about retiring..."

"We are retired. This is our retirement plan, remember?"

"I remember all right," she snapped, her voice increasing in volume. "I just wonder whether it might be time for a rethink. Shouldn't retirement involve less work? And if I am going to work, couldn't it be taking care of my grandchildren?"

"It could be if they didn't live hundreds of miles away from us."

"Or if we didn't live hundreds of miles from them," Flora said pointedly.

"Let's not start this again," Rodney replied. "I know you miss them, but we'd hate living in a city. Besides, we've got a good thing going here. It's what we always dreamed of."

Flora's voice lowered in volume again, becoming hard to make out. "I didn't dream of rearranging my furniture to suit the whims of some spoiled little princess."

"Indulge her in her photoshoot," Rodney said. "She'll be gone in a few days and when she writes us a glowing review, all the furniture removal will be worth it."

Flora didn't have a chance to argue since the sound of footsteps interrupted them.

Vinny strode along the hallway, casting Lily a cursory glance before stopping at the doorway to the breakfast room.

"Everything okay?" Rodney asked, stepping closer to Vinny and subsequently into Lily's field of vision. "Can we help you with anything else out there? Drinks maybe?"

"Did one of you move my camera?" Vinny asked accusingly. "It was out there on the table and now it's vanished."

"It can't have just vanished," Rodney said. "Maybe it got moved while we were rearranging things. I'll come and help you look."

"It's not exactly small," Vinny pointed out. "If it was out there, I'd have found it myself."

"Maybe someone moved it inside out of the way." Rodney patted Vinny's shoulder. "Let's have a proper look around."

Placated, Vinny followed him, and Lily descended the rest of the stairs.

"Everything okay?" Flora said, stepping into the hallway.

"Great, thank you. I'm just off for a bit of exploring."

"Lovely weather for it," Flora said.

Yes, Lily thought. *Perfect weather for an ice cream.*

If only she could find the shop.

Chapter Two

SALTY AIR RUSHED AROUND LILY, invigorating her on her walk across the island. Green fields and privet hedges gave the sense that a piece of the English countryside had been dropped into the Atlantic Ocean. At least until the water came into view. Given the azure hue it felt more like Caribbean waters than the Atlantic. The sun slipped out from a fluffy cloud, seeming to rain diamonds on the surface of the rippling waves.

With her senses fixed on her surroundings, it felt like no time until Lily reached Hugh Town. After strolling along the quaint main street, bordered by dainty shops, she found the harbour and then Porthcressa beach, which stretched in a long crescent.

At the top of the beach, a concrete promenade was dotted with cafes and outdoor seating. No sign of an ice cream shop, though.

A dog and its owner veered around her as she pulled her backpack from her shoulder. After retrieving her photo, she studied it as though she hadn't already looked at it a thousand times.

Lily could only have been around four when it was taken.

Presumably it was one of the last photos of their little family – and one of the few Lily had of the three of them.

It should have been a treasured possession when she was growing up, but she'd only recently found it among her uncle's things. Strange that he'd never shown it to her before, especially as she'd asked him on several occasions about one of her only clear memories of her parents – of being in an ice cream shop where the owner had taken her inside and shown her how the ice cream was made in huge metal machines.

Her uncle had brushed her questions about it aside until she'd convinced herself it wasn't a real memory at all. At least until she'd found the photo and been convinced it was taken at the ice cream shop from her memories.

The building in the photo was at the end of the row, but as she set off in that direction she felt a sinking feeling. An ice cream shop would surely have a buzz of people. There was nothing of the sort here. In fact, the last building was derelict and a sorry sight given its prime beach location.

Maybe she wasn't even in the right place. Turning in a circle, she wondered why she was even looking for an ice cream shop that she'd visited with her parents more than twenty years ago. The chances of it still being in operation had been slim, and what exactly had she intended to do when she'd found it?

Ripping her gaze from the building, she stared out to sea and felt an emptiness settle in her stomach. The hunt for the ice cream shop had given her a purpose, and if this was the end of that road, what would she do next? Where would she go?

Home, presumably. She just wasn't sure where that was.

Not one for self-pity, she told herself to get a grip and returned her attention to the rundown old building.

The wind seemed to stop and the noise of seagulls and waves and holidaymakers faded as a shiver crept up Lily's spine and brought goosebumps rippling over the back of her neck. She'd been there before; she was sure of it.

Generally, she was too level-headed to believe in anything otherwordly, but she had the distinct notion she'd just crossed paths with a past version of herself.

A deep inhale brought everything back into focus at the exact moment that a wild gust whipped at her hair and tore the photograph from her fingers.

It sailed with the wind, then landed squarely on the chest of a young guy sauntering along the promenade. He grinned as he caught it and gave a flick of his head to sweep his hair aside.

"That was some gust," he said. "Is this yours?"

"Yes. Thank you." She went to retrieve the photo from his outstretched hand, but he stopped before she could take it and withdrew slightly, eyes dropping to the picture.

He squinted at the photo as he finally passed it to Lily. "Is that the old ice cream shop?"

Her brain stalled and all she could do was stare at him. He was oddly familiar with his sandy brown hair and smiling eyes. She guessed he'd be in his mid-twenties – the same as her.

"Sorry," he said. "There used to be an ice cream shop here, and the photo kind of looks like it."

"Yes." Like a puppy begging for attention, Lily offered the photo back to him. "That's what I was trying to work out. I've been trying to find out where the photo was taken." She flicked her thumb toward the building. "So this *was* an ice cream shop?"

"Yeah." His eyes sparkled as he studied the photo. "I only have vague memories of the place but my older brothers talked about it a lot. The owner used to make the ice cream on the premises, and would give little tours so you could see how the ice cream was made."

"So I didn't imagine it," she said wistfully, a feeling of triumph washing over her. "I had memories of the place but I was never sure if it was a real memory."

"I know that feeling. Sometimes I mention something from my childhood to my mum and my brothers and they all deny any knowledge of it. I don't know if they genuinely don't remember or if they're just winding me up." He grinned. "I'm the baby of the family so I sometimes feel as though I had a completely different childhood to my brothers."

"I don't have siblings," she muttered, feeling an immediate connection to the guy and wondering again at the familiarity of his features.

"This is a great photo," he said, handing it back. "You and your parents, I take it?"

"Yes." She smothered the urge to tell him that they hadn't lived long enough for her to really know them. "I don't know why I was so keen to find this place. Looking for a bit of nostalgia, I suppose. Do you know when it closed?"

He puffed his cheeks out. "It must have been twenty years ago. There was a fire so it closed for a while. I don't think they reopened after that. Shame because it must have been a gold mine. Prime location..."

His words suddenly felt faraway, and Lily's gaze drifted to the building. "A fire?" she murmured, her brain whirring.

"I think they got it under control quickly. There was no damage to the structure of the building but... are you okay?"

She swallowed hard. It was natural that any mention of fire triggered memories of her parents. This was a weird coincidence, that was all. Her parents had died in a fire and this place had also had a fire. Both had taken place in Cornwall, but in very different locations since their family home had been in Truro. Forcing her mind back to the present, she smiled at the young guy with friendly features.

"No one wanted to buy the building?" she asked, finding it hard to believe it had stood empty for all those years.

"Oh, *people* would love to buy it." He tilted his head, eyes crinkling at the corners as he chuckled. "I've been trying to get my hands on it for a while. A few years ago I decided it was the perfect business opportunity and attempted to track down the owner."

"And?" she asked eagerly.

"Apparently they don't want to be found. I managed to speak to a solicitor acting on their behalf but I couldn't get much out of him. Only that it wasn't for sale. They wouldn't even let me lease it."

Lily frowned, her gaze lingering on the stone building. "That's weird. Why not rent it out and make money from it? Like you say, it's in the perfect spot with so much passing trade."

"Yes!" His eyes lit up. "And it still has all the old ice cream making equipment in there. Those machines are solid. I'd bet anything they still work." His eyebrows drew together. "I only know that from peering in the back windows, and I was technically trespassing so you didn't get that information from me."

Lily beamed at his playful tone. "So you don't know what happened to the owner?"

"She moved back to the mainland." He scratched at his jaw. "If you want more information you could always ask the solicitor. Mr Greaves' office is just over on Silver Street. But remember, if this place ever comes on the market, I've got first dibs."

She let out a gentle laugh at the sparkle in his eyes. "Don't worry. I have no plans to get into the ice cream business. I'm only here for a week."

"Well I hope you have a good week." He took a step away from her. "I'm Kit, by the way. I own the tourist train that runs around the island."

"I read about that." She recalled the flyer in her room with his smiling face on it. So that was why he felt so familiar. "It looks fun."

His lips twitched at the corners. "It's the number one rated thing to do on St Mary's. Definitely not to be missed."

"I'll check it out," she told him, raising a hand to wave as he backed away.

Turning back to the shop, she sucked in a deep breath. She'd found it. And her memories were real.

And the fact that there'd been a fire was just a coincidence. Wasn't it?

Now, more than ever, she longed to speak to her uncle.

Dropping dead of a heart attack in his mid-fifties, leaving her all alone in the world and with a bunch of unanswered questions about her childhood, had been very inconsiderate of him.

Chapter Three

AFTER A QUICK LUNCH in a cafe by the harbour, Lily made the gentle walk back across the island. Approaching the bed and breakfast, she spotted the gardener, Oscar, standing beside the low stone wall. With his head bent, he chatted to a girl around his age. Her sweep of long dark hair cast her face in shadow, intensifying her scowl as she spoke in a rush. She jabbed Oscar in the centre of his chest, punctuating whatever she was saying. Slowing her pace, Lily waited for them to notice her.

"He's a creep," Oscar snarled. "We should go to the police and tell them everything. He should be locked up."

"I don't care about that," the girl said. "I just want—" Her head snapped to Lily. "Hi," she said, her features softening.

"Hello." Oscar rocked back on his heels and stepped casually away from his friend. "Have you been exploring the island?"

Lily nodded and moved automatically to the garden gate. "I had a wander around Hugh Town and got some lunch. Did the guy's camera turn up?"

Oscar's cheeks pinked, and he shifted his weight from one foot to the other while his friend took a sudden interest in the gravel by her feet, pushing a couple of loose stones with the toe of her scuffed trainer.

"Not yet," Oscar said. "He thinks someone might have slipped into the garden and stolen it, but we were all here and no one saw anything."

"I'm sure it will turn up," the girl said. "I better go." She glared at Oscar, then wandered away down the lane.

"It's a work camera," Oscar said, leaning against the wall, then immediately straightening up again. "I guess that's why he's freaking out. He needs it for the job. He takes photos for Alanna's blog. She's kind of famous, I think. I hadn't heard of her but Katie follows her blog." He tipped his head in the direction of his retreating friend.

"Hopefully he just put it down somewhere without thinking," Lily remarked. "I do that with keys a lot."

Oscar cast a glance at the house. "Flora called the police to report it. Which seems premature if you ask me, but she said when it comes to guests she has to do everything correctly. Vinny's not happy, though. He says he doesn't want to spend his time dealing with the bizzies. He seems to have an issue with police in general. But then..."

"What?" Lily asked, jutting her chin out.

"Nothing." He waved a hand dismissively. "I guess no one wants to have to deal with the police on holiday, even if it is a working holiday."

"Yeah."

Oscar's eyebrows drew quickly together. "We don't usually have problems like this. Thefts and whatnot. There's hardly any crime on the island. As you can tell by the fact that the police officer arrived ten minutes after Flora called. They're not exactly snowed under with work."

"The police are already here?" Lily asked.

"Yes. Out in the garden. The scene of the crime." His eyes flashed mockingly.

Lily took steps along the front path. "I didn't think staying in a quiet little bed and breakfast would include so much drama."

"It's honestly not usually like this." He tipped his head in a farewell gesture when she reached the front door.

Inside, the sound of raised voices drifted along the hallway. Slipping straight upstairs, Lily placed her backpack on the bed before tiptoeing to the window to reclaim her viewing spot.

Down in the garden, the small group stood around the table on the patio – Alanna and Marc at one side, and Flora and Rodney on the other. The uniformed police officer held court at the head of the table, his gaze following Vinny, who paced like a bee buzzing around the group.

Curiosity had Lily reaching for the window handle. The modern window frames opened soundlessly, and the scene below was immediately unmuted.

"I don't want to make a fuss, that's all," Vinny was saying, his tone rough with anger. "There's no need to make a report or anything. It'll probably turn up with a thorough search."

The officer continued to try and pin Vinny with his gaze. "It's not a problem. Mrs Miller said there'd already been a thorough search. I can take a statement. Then I can put an alert out to the staff at the airport and ferry to keep an eye out for anything suspicious. You'll also need a police report to file an insurance claim."

"I don't have time for all this," Vinny said, waving an arm.

"It's not as though you can do any work without your camera," Alanna pointed out, with a dramatic sigh.

"Sorry to have bothered you," Vinny said to the officer. "I really think the camera will turn up. There was no need to waste your time."

Flora smoothed down a lock of frizzy grey hair by her temple as she cleared her throat. "I don't think it's wasting time. If there's been a theft, it needs to be properly reported, and the thief caught. It reflects badly on our business otherwise."

"It's hardly our fault," her husband put in, propping his hands on his narrow hips, making him appear even more gangly.

"I know that, but it doesn't stop people from writing bad reviews, does it?" Flora said, quietly enough that Lily could only just make out her words.

"There was no chance of you getting a good review from me, anyway." Finally, Vinny stopped his pacing. "Not after that breakfast this morning. You realise you're supposed to stop cooking bacon before it turns black?"

Lily pressed her lips together to stop herself from laughing. He was right though; the breakfast hadn't been great.

"The bed's bloody uncomfortable, too," Vinny continued to rant. "I realise the description of the place is only bed and breakfast but there's an expectation that the bed will be at least reasonably comfy and the breakfast edible." He shook his head. "At least it won't be difficult to come up with a heading for my review – Terrible bed and even worse breakfast!"

While Rodney jumped to the defence of his wife's cooking with an excuse about a fault in the stovetop, Lily's gaze fell to the officer who slid his fingers around the back of his neck to massage the muscles and muss up his dark hair while he was at it.

He looked bored out of his mind. The slight shadow under his eyes hinted at a lack of sleep, and there was something about the way he winced at the increasing volume of the group that gave Lily the impression he might be nursing a hangover.

Her eyes were still on him when he lifted his gaze to her window. Freezing in place, she locked eyes with him as his eyebrows drew together. Then he was back to the situation in front of him, holding out his palms as he urged everyone to settle down.

"I'm sure the breakfast will be better tomorrow," he said. "Why don't you all take some time to calm down? If the camera still hasn't turned up by tomorrow I'll write up an official report."

"I'm sure that won't be necessary," Vinny grumbled. "But thanks for coming out."

"Yes, thank you so much, PC Grainger," Flora said, following him around the side of the house with her husband in tow.

The other three stayed in the garden, Marc taking a seat while Alanna and Vinny remained standing.

"I guess you can't have your photo shoot," Marc said, eyes flicking to the two-seater couch and coffee table which adorned the far corner of the garden.

"I can use my phone," Vinny said with an irritated shake of the head.

"You should probably have a backup camera," Alanna said. "I'm not paying you to take photos on your phone. I could just as well get Marc to take them."

"You're enjoying this, aren't you?" Vinny snarled, his tone and posture full of menace. "Was it you? Did you take my camera?"

"Why would I take your camera?" she asked with a roll of her eyes.

"It just seems a bit suss that you keep threatening to replace me, and then my camera goes missing."

Marc drummed his fingers on the table in front of him. "Calm down," he said to Vinny. "You know Alanna didn't touch your camera. Getting all worked up about it isn't going to help find it."

"Someone must have taken it," Alanna said, negating her boyfriend's attempt to quell Vinny's agitation.

Vinny looked thoughtful as he set off pacing again. "Where's that scrawny young lad? I ought to ask him."

"Why would he steal your camera from right under your nose?" Alanna asked.

"I don't know, but he could have easily done it." As his

eyes darted around, they came up to the window and snagged on Lily before she could move out of the way. "What are you staring at?" he bellowed.

As she instinctively retreated, the voices outside faded until all was quiet. The stillness didn't last long, broken by the sound of footsteps pounding up the stairs.

With a feeling of trepidation, Lily stared at the door.

The wood shuddered slightly when someone banged on the other side of it.

Chapter Four

With both of his colleagues out of action due to illness, PC Flynn Grainger had been left in charge of the Isles of Scilly police station. Generally, there'd be a sergeant and a PC for the group of islands with just over two thousand residents, but it turned out the archipelago was a convenient place to squirrel away a police officer who needed to be out of the way for a while. So Flynn was now the third member of the team.

Since he hadn't technically done anything wrong, this wasn't officially a punishment, but Flynn could hardly have felt more caged if he'd been locked in a cell.

His job had been his passion for the nine years he'd spent in the force. Even before then, actually – he'd wanted to join the police for as long as he could remember. Initially, it was to make his dad proud, but when it became clear that would never happen, he was still devoted to his profession.

He loved the feeling that he was doing something worthwhile. That he could help people.

Then there was the adrenaline rush which came with every call.

Or with every call he'd got working for the Met. On the quaint Isles of Scilly, he'd yet to experience that rush. Emergency calls didn't seem to be a thing out here in the Atlantic. The sleepy group of islands felt like something from an Enid Blyton novel. He was certain four kids and their dog could keep the peace on the Scillies, no problem at all.

Community policing was not what he'd joined the force for. And given that his sergeant was livid at having Flynn around, there really wasn't any policing for him to do at all. He'd been assigned to a desk for the most part. He was the unofficial admin for the Isles of Scilly Police social media page. Which got a surprising amount of traffic. The community hub, or so it seemed. If someone had a problem with their neighbour, or their bins, or a grievance with badly parked vehicles, they expressed it on the social media page. So the reality was that he hadn't even been demoted to community policing, but the policing of an online neighbourhood watch. Where there was virtually nothing of interest to watch.

It meant that, left alone to hold the fort, he felt a buzz of excitement at the phone call from the owner of a bed and breakfast on the island. Mrs Miller didn't go into details, just reported that there was an issue with one of her guests and requested that someone call by to help resolve the issue.

There was something about not knowing what he was going to that had his adrenaline pumping as he drove across the island. It hadn't sounded at all urgent, but it was something. And something he'd need to deal with alone.

The adrenaline supply was immediately cut off when he reached the house to find he'd been called out to a report of a stolen camera. Or quite possibly just a lost camera. And a bunch of squabbling adults acting like children.

He'd have preferred it if the squabbling had turned physical. A fist fight would get his blood pumping. As it was, the petty arguing made his head pound, reminding him he'd had several pints too many the previous evening. He'd also taken some blonde back to his place and, if he recalled correctly, he hadn't been discreet in leaving the pub with her.

Forcing his brain to the present, he tried his best to smooth tempers, and offered to provide a report for the guy who'd misplaced his camera. He declined, and PC Grainger felt an odd weariness at the thought that he wouldn't have minded the paperwork. That's how bad things were.

When his gaze flicked to the upstairs window, he found a pair of eyes on him. The woman with chestnut brown hair drew her chin in as though she wanted to withdraw from view but knew she'd left it too late to avoid being noticed. He held her gaze, then returned to the chatter in front of him.

After wrapping things up, he left thinking that they'd wasted his time.

It was a waste of his training, and being on the islands was a waste of his life.

He lingered on the lane at the front of the house, pacing and cursing and wishing he were anywhere in the world but there.

With his mind so distracted, he almost didn't catch the raised voices inside. His ears pricked up, listening.

It wasn't the bickering he'd previously encountered. This was pure anger.

Adrenaline kicked in again. From one moment to the next Flynn went from feeling adrift, to being exactly where he was supposed to be.

Chapter Five

In three strides, Lily crossed the room and yanked the door open, putting an end to the banging.

"What are you doing?" she asked, glaring at Vinny.

His cheek twitched and he looked slightly disconcerted, as though he'd expected her to be intimidated. "Have you seen my camera? Someone stole it."

"Maybe you've just misplaced it," she suggested.

"It's a bloody big camera. It'd be hard not to spot, and we've looked everywhere."

"I haven't seen it," she said. "But I'll keep an eye out."

He stuck his arm out, blocking her attempt to close the door. "If you don't know anything about it, you won't mind me taking a quick look around in here." It wasn't a question and he didn't wait for a response as he barged past her.

It took a moment for Lily to find words, but when she did, they were slow and full of venom. "You need to get out, right now."

"After I've had a quick check." He went to her open suitcase and rummaged through it, slinging a few items of clothing around as he did.

"What the hell is wrong with you?" Lily shouted. "Get out of my stuff and out of the room."

"I need the camera." Like a man possessed, he flung open the wardrobe doors, only to find it empty. When he moved to the desk and pulled out one drawer after another, Lily's anger levels went through the roof, then spiked when his eyes landed on the photo in the centre of the desk. "Cute picture," he drawled menacingly.

"If you touch anything else in here, I'll break your arm." He'd crossed a line the moment he'd entered her room and she'd struggle to control her rage for much longer.

His grin was of the taunting variety as his hand moved purposefully to the photo. Slowly, he held it up in front of him. "What were you going to break? My arm, was it?"

Lowering her gaze, she shook her head. She caught his cocky expression in the second before she lunged at him.

The photo fluttered to the floor when she grabbed his wrist and twisted his arm behind his back. He yelped like a puppy who'd had their tail stepped on.

If she twisted any further, she'd no doubt hear the crack of bone or tendons or both.

"I told you not to touch my stuff," she whispered in his ear before releasing him with a shove.

He clutched his arm to his chest.

"Is everything all right in here?"

Lily's gaze snapped to the door and the police officer, who was taller up close.

"I heard raised voices," he said, with a subtle tilt of the head.

"That psychopath just attacked me." Vinny pointed at Lily – an unnecessary gesture since there was no one else around. "Almost snapped my arm. You need to arrest her."

The officer looked bored. "So you don't want to report your stolen camera but you'd like to press charges for assault?"

"Yes. I bloody would."

"You're claiming *she* assaulted you?" His gaze travelled over Lily and she forced herself not to fidget under the scrutiny of his bright blue eyes.

"You must have seen her," Vinny snapped.

"Me?" He blew out a breath. "I just heard shouting and came to investigate. I'm happy to take a statement, though."

Lily opened her mouth to object, but he spoke over her.

"Firstly, I need to know whose room this is." His features were neutral as he looked at Lily and then at Vinny.

"It's my room," Lily stated. "And he——"

The officer cut her off. "So she invited you in here?" he asked Vinny.

"Well, I... um..." Vinny's cheeks flushed a deep red. "I wanted to look for my camera," he spluttered.

The officer's eyes narrowed as he looked questioningly at Lily. "I didn't catch your name..."

"Lily," she told him. "Lily Larkin."

"Lily said that was okay?" he went on, his gaze back to Vinny. "She agreed you could come in here and look for your camera?"

While Vinny did a perfect goldfish impression, Lily suppressed a grin.

The police officer gave a subtle shrug. "Because if you entered her room without permission, I'm not sure your accusation of assault is going to hold up. Especially as it's going to be your word against Lily's."

"You must have seen her?" he said, a definite edge of panic in his voice.

"I didn't see anything. I just heard shouting and came up here to find you uninvited in this woman's room. Now, I'm wondering if Lily would like to make a complaint about you..." His gaze slid to her.

"I just want him out of my room," she said.

"I'm going," Vinny huffed.

The officer stood aside, then watched Vinny cross the landing.

"Thank you," Lily said.

Again, the officer shrugged, his eyes showing no emotion whatsoever.

It wasn't just that he looked bored by his job, Lily realised. He looked like someone who was bored by life. Like he was going through the motions without taking any real interest in anything.

"Does this work?" he asked, tapping the lock on her door.

"Yeah."

"Make sure you use it. And if he gives you any more trouble, call the station." He pulled a card from one of many pockets in his black stab vest.

Taking it, she looked for his name, but it only contained the address and phone number for the Isles of Scilly police station. "Thanks... officer...?"

"It's PC." His small smile brightened his features. "Flynn Grainger."

Chapter Six

FOLLOWING the incident with Vinny that afternoon, Lily hadn't been keen to hang around the B&B. She headed back out to explore a few of St. Mary's beaches and after a couple of hours of aimless wandering, she ended up in the pub at the harbour for dinner.

Having finished her meal, Lily remained sitting at the bar. The pub had a nautical theme, with shipping and fishing artefacts decorating every inch of space. It was a feast for the eyes, but Lily kept her focus on her phone, pretending to be engrossed so she could listen in on a nearby conversation without being noticed.

"He's an absolute disgrace," the red-headed barmaid was saying to the young woman opposite her. "You can't be a policeman in a small community and act like that."

"He's off duty," her friend replied across the bar. "Surely he can do what he wants. It's not as though there's a law about police officers getting drunk and sleeping around... as long as it's on their own time."

The barmaid leaned on the bar. "It seems very unprofessional to me."

"Because you're used to squeaky clean Sergeant Proctor."

"They couldn't be more different, could they?" The barmaid's gaze shifted across the room to where PC Grainger was sitting at a table for two with a pint in front of him and a slender young blonde opposite him. Their hands met on the table and the woman pawed at the back of his fingers like an attention-hungry feline.

"How does he do it anyway?" the barmaid asked, lowering her voice even further. "That's the third woman I've seen him with and he's only been on the island for a month."

"Do you think it might be because he's gorgeous?" the woman asked mockingly. "It could also be something to do with the uniform."

"He's not in uniform now," the barmaid pointed out. "And I don't think he's that good looking."

"Are you serious?" The woman's voice rose before she caught herself and switched back to hushed tones. "He's stunning. The colour of his eyes is insane."

"Fine, he's fit, but his personality is sadly lacking."

The friend, sitting just a couple of bar stools over from Lily, grinned mischievously. "I'd guess his lady friend this evening isn't overly concerned by his conversational skills."

"True." The barmaid straightened up and glanced again at PC Grainger. Almost immediately she leaned back on the bar. "I didn't even tell you the latest rumour about him..."

"Which lucky person are you gossiping about now?" a loud male voice cut in.

Recognising the voice, Lily automatically looked up.

"Oh, hello!" he said, catching her eye.

"Hi." She ignored the other two sets of eyes on her. "Kit, wasn't it?"

"Yes. I don't think I caught your name." He held his hand out and Lily introduced herself.

"You've met my girlfriend, I take it..." He indicated the barmaid. "Seren."

Lily smiled awkwardly.

"I met Lily earlier," Kit said. "Checking out the site of the old ice cream shop."

"I loved that place," Seren said, before being interrupted by her friend who leaned in Lily's direction.

"I'm Keira," she told Lily.

"My brother's girlfriend," Kit added.

"It's quite the family get together," Lily remarked.

"Hardly," Keira said. "The place would be heaving if all Kit's family was in here. There are loads of them. You can't throw a stone on this island without hitting a member of the Treneary family."

"You should really stop throwing stones at my family," Kit said dryly, earning himself a punch on the arm from Keira.

"Anyway," she said to Lily with a gentle grimace. "Sorry if we were talking loudly before..."

"You weren't, but I may have been eavesdropping a little."

"Sorry about these two," Kit said. "They're a right pair of gossips."

"We don't usually gossip like that," Keira said, causing Kit to choke on a laugh.

"We don't!" She aimed a playful elbow at his ribs. "But it's not every day a hot copper turns up on the island. It's caused quite a stir. Especially as he seems intent on sleeping with every single woman he meets."

"Is he hot?" Kit asked, with a comical frown.

"He's pretty easy on the eyes," Keira said. "But don't tell Noah I said that."

"I suppose he's sort of classically handsome." Kit raised an eyebrow. "I didn't think women were into that these days."

"Classically handsome men?" Seren said, the corners of her lips twitching. "No. I don't think women like that at all."

"I thought rugged good looks were all the rage." Kit lifted his chin a fraction. "If you're telling me classically handsome is back in, I might have to rethink my haircut."

Beside him, Keira snorted a laugh.

"What's so funny?" he demanded.

"Nothing." She beamed and reached out to pinch his cheek. "You're so cute."

"Hey." He swatted her hand away. "That's what the old ladies tell me. When I take the seniors from the nursing home out for a train ride, all I hear is how cute I am. I assumed it was bad eyesight that made them mistake my rugged good looks for cuteness."

Keira opened her mouth to comment then pressed her lips together at the last moment.

"Seren likes my rugged good looks, anyway," he said firmly.

"I do." Seren's smile was full of affection. "Very much."

They were a cute couple, Lily thought before her gaze drifted across the room again.

"It is all a bit mysterious, isn't it?" Kit said. "There was definitely no opening for another PC on the island. And Sergent Proctor's very shifty if you ask him about it. Though he did say PC Grainger was probably only here on a temporary posting."

"I met him today." Lily's words drew the attention of all three of them. "PC Grainger," she clarified.

"Did he try to sleep with you?" Keira asked.

"No." She laughed at their eager faces.

"What happened?" Kit asked with a mischievous grin. "Tell us everything."

"You've got a cheek calling us gossips," Keira told him affectionately.

"Tell us," Seren said across the bar.

Lily's gaze lingered on PC Grainger, who was completely oblivious to being the centre of their conversation. Then she flicked her eyes back across the bar. "First I want to know what you were about to say. About a rumour..."

"I heard he was working in London." Seren's whispered words had them all leaning in. "He got caught sleeping with

34

some police chief's daughter... she was only young... seventeen, I think. It was a big scandal but not actually a sackable offence. They've sent him over here to keep him out of the way while the dust settles."

"I don't believe it," Keira said. "It sounds totally made up."

"Sounds believable to me," Seren said. "I've seen him leave this place with three different women since he's been here."

"It's weird that you're keeping track of his conquests," Kit said with a small shake of his head.

"There are probably more," Seren said idly. "His loose morals aren't my only issue with him. You need to be friendly for small town policing and I'm not sure he knows the meaning of the word. He's borderline rude when I serve him. And he never tips." She looked at Lily. "What did you make of him?"

Before she could answer, Kit spoke. "I thought you were only visiting... how have you already met our new constable?"

She gave them a rundown of her strange day at the B&B, excluding the minor detail of her manhandling Vinny, but finishing with PC Grainger arriving in her room.

"He sounds quite heroic," Seren said grudgingly.

"I don't know about that," Lily said. "I was glad he turned up when he did, though."

"This won't be good for Flora and Rodney." Kit's eyes were fixed on his phone. "The guy's already written them a review."

"What does it say?" Keira asked.

He pursed his lips as his eyes darted over the screen. "Nothing about the camera. It's mostly about the breakfast." His lips twitched upwards. "He has a real bee in his bonnet about his overcooked bacon. And then he rants about the bed and the pillow." Kit paused and chuckled. "It's quite clever not to mention the camera. A theft might not put people off since it would sound like a one-off and not the owner's fault. But improperly cooked bacon..." He wiggled his eyebrows. "That's got to be the most damaging complaint for a B&B."

"My theory about Flora was wrong anyway," Seren said. "I really thought she'd been writing the bad reviews herself."

"Why would she do that?" Keira asked, voicing the question on the tip of Lily's tongue.

Kit tilted his head to one side. "She and Rodney were in here last week. Rodney was complaining about a spate of bad reviews and some cancelled bookings. Flora jokingly said that it might be time to move to the mainland. Except it didn't really sound like a joke. I mentioned it to Mum and she said she wouldn't be surprised. Apparently, Flora has been desperate to move closer to her grandchildren for a couple of years now."

"I heard her mention that today too," Lily told them.

Kit returned his phone to his pocket. "Rodney would never leave St. Mary's."

"That's why I thought she might have been the one writing the reviews," Seren said. "If the business goes under they might have no choice but to sell up and leave."

Keira stared at her. "You have a worryingly suspicious mind. People generally aren't that devious."

"Maybe she isn't writing fake reviews," Lily mused. "But she could be the *reason* they're getting the reviews..."

"You think she burned the bacon on purpose?" Kit said.

Lily shrugged. "Maybe."

"Ooh!" Seren's eyes widened and she lowered her voice to a whisper. "Maybe it was her who stole the camera!"

Keira's burst of laughter cut through the atmosphere. "You sound like a bunch of conspiracy theorists! Flora Miller hasn't turned to crime."

"It actually sounds quite believable to me." Seren looked at Kit. "Do you think we watch too many crime dramas?"

He wrinkled his nose. "Maybe."

Over the next hour, Lily enjoyed the light-hearted chatter and banter with her three new friends. At one point she considered raising the subject of the ice cream shop again.

Only briefly though – until she realised that for the first time in a long time she felt utterly relaxed. She was enjoying being sociable and that certainly wasn't a regular occurrence for her.

After six months of being consumed by the idea of finding the ice cream shop, it felt good to be distracted.

She knew herself well enough to know she wouldn't be able to put it out of her mind indefinitely.

But at least for the evening, she was putting the mystery of the ice cream shop aside.

Chapter Seven

SUNDAY

ON HER SECOND morning on St Mary's, Lily woke to the sound of rain pelting the window like hundreds of tiny bullets. The noise died off as the wind changed direction but she was fully awake, a gentle headache informing her she shouldn't have had that third glass of wine in the Mermaid Inn.

Lying in bed, listening to the rain, her thoughts were once again on the ice cream shop. A weariness seemed to pin her to the bed but she knew she couldn't drop her enquiries just yet. She'd visit the solicitor Kit had mentioned, and if he couldn't tell her anything more, she was determined to set it aside and move on with her life.

That would mean figuring out what to do with her life, of course.

With a frustrated growl, she tossed the bedclothes aside and stretched as she stood. A run should help clear her head. After pulling on her jogging gear, she listened at the door to check the coast was clear. The last thing she wanted was another encounter with Vinny. When she was confident there was no one around, she set off out of the house.

The weather should probably have dissuaded her from her early morning jog, but the rain and wind had stopped by the time she stepped outside. Now, a low-hanging fog gave the deserted lanes an eerie quality that pushed Lily to run at a faster pace than usual. She didn't see a soul until she reached Hugh Town where a few people gave life to the main street.

It wasn't as though she expected to find the solicitor's office open at that time, and especially not on a Sunday, but she ended up standing in front of it, nonetheless. Shaking her head, she chastised herself again for getting obsessed with an ice cream shop from her childhood. There was no significance to the place, she told herself, trying to override the voice in her head that said there was a reason the memory had stayed with her.

After a deep inhale, she continued on her way, opting for a gentler pace as she joined the coastal path for her final stretch back towards the B&B. The early morning stillness made her uneasy, and she was glad when the silence was broken by the screech of gulls who didn't appear to be any more impressed than she was by the fog hanging out over the water and shrouding the path in front of her.

It got suddenly denser before clearing again, and the sound of Lily's trainers pounding the path seemed to echo all around. Trying to ignore the rushing in her ears, she concentrated on the uneven path, sure that any moment now, the B&B would come into view.

Rounding the next bend, a short stretch of golden sand greeted her and the surroundings became familiar. It was the beach which she could see from her window at the B&B. At the far end of the beach, colossal boulders loomed ominously. Still, Lily felt more at ease now that she knew where she was. A little further and she'd be back at the house.

Instead of veering up to the lane, she remained on the

sandy path, slowing her pace to walk over the sand to the shoreline. The water, which had been such an inviting shade of turquoise the previous day, was dark and unwelcoming now. She dragged the zip of her hoodie up to her chin and heaved in huge lungfuls of sea air as the damp sand shifted under her weight. At the far end of the beach, she took a moment to watch the water gently lapping at the rocks.

A dark shape caught her eye just as she was turning away.

"It's nothing," she said, trying to quell the primal part of her that was on alert for a threat. The fog and the dim morning light were playing tricks on her mind, she was sure of it.

Despite her trepidation, she walked forwards, stepping onto the rocks beneath the imposing boulders. Squinting, she tried to make out exactly what she was looking at. Probably some washed up piece of rubbish.

The closer she got, the more frenzied her heart beat became. She wasn't sure when she admitted to herself that her eyes weren't playing tricks on her.

And that what she was seeing was a body lying face down in a rock pool.

Chapter Eight

THE COMPUTER SCREEN in front of PC Grainger showed the social media page for the station. He'd been replying to a post about inconveniently parked golf buggies before he'd zoned out.

Now, the shrill ring of the phone snapped him from his trance. Expecting it to be a call following up on the golf cart situation, he hesitated before answering.

"Scilly police station," he said, rubbing the creases on his forehead. "PC Grainger speaking."

"Hi," the soft female voice said, an air of confusion to the single syllable.

Flynn frowned. "Can I help?"

"I... um..."

Something in her stuttering made him sit up straighter. "Can you give me your name?"

"Lily," she said. "You gave me your card yesterday."

"At the bed and breakfast?"

"Yeah."

He thought back to the guy who'd been in her room. She'd seemed in full control of the situation, leaving little room for him to play hero, but knowing that the guy had barged into her

43

room left him feeling uneasy. He'd seen Vinny's type so many times before. Misogynistic bullies through and through.

"Is that guy bothering you again?" he asked.

"No." Her voice quivered and he had the feeling she was outdoors. A hush of wind or waves or both filled the silence. "I don't think he'll be bothering anyone ever again."

Her voice was so quiet, Flynn could barely make out the words. "Excuse me?"

"He's dead," she said flatly.

"He's *what?*"

"I *think* he's dead." Her words came in a rush now. "There's blood. A lot of blood... it's in the water too. The rock pool is filled with blood. Also, he's twisted at a weird angle."

PC Grainger was on his feet in an instant. "Where are you?"

"I'm not sure. Should I do something? I'm fairly sure he's dead, but should I try to help him?"

"Look around and tell me what you can see. You said there are rock pools?"

"I'm near the bed and breakfast. By the water."

"Are you okay? Are you hurt at all?" His mind conjured a variety of scenarios which could have led to the guy bleeding in a rock pool. All of them made him concerned about Lily's welfare.

"I'm fine," she said. "I was out for a run and I saw him lying on the rocks. I'm sure he's dead. His face is in the water and there's a lot of blood..." She made a nauseated grunt. "Like I said, he's all twisted... his arm and his leg."

"Don't look," he told her, knowing how these things could etch themselves on your brain. At least it didn't sound as though there'd been any sort of altercation.

Ending the call felt wrong, but they were on the landline and he couldn't do anything while still on the phone with her. "I'm going to put you on hold for a moment," he told her. "Just hang on a minute."

After putting her on hold, he felt a jolt of frustration. He didn't know the procedure for anything on this stupid island. In London, he'd have got the call from a dispatcher and would be on his way there already.

Grabbing his walkie-talkie, he gave his badge number and then relayed the situation to the dispatcher. They informed him it'd be easier for him to call the medics himself, but that they'd try to get in touch with his sergeant.

"The system is ridiculous," he muttered to himself while searching for the number for the island's hospital. Once he'd spoken to someone there and given them a location, he got back on the phone to Lily.

"I'm on the way," he told her. "Stay where you are."

He dragged his stab vest on, snatched up his walkie-talkie and coat, then bolted out of the door and almost collided with the sergeant coming the other way. Graham Proctor lived in the house right beside the station. His hair was stuck at an odd angle and the missed button on his shirt announced that he'd got dressed in a rush. He stopped and coughed fiercely before catching his breath.

"What the hell is going on? I had a call from dispatch about a dead body."

"Yes." Flynn nodded curtly. "Near the Miller's bed and breakfast. I was called out there yesterday so I know where it is."

Sergeant Proctor blinked in confusion. "Who's the corpse?"

"A guy staying at the Miller's place."

"Old?"

"No. Young. Twenties, I guess. Maybe thirty."

After another coughing fit, the sergeant shook his head. "People don't just die around here."

"Maybe someone should have told him that." Impatiently, Flynn stepped around him to get in the car. "Are you coming?"

"Dispatch said it wasn't an emergency call... someone called the station?"

"Yeah." He paused with the driver's door open. "So?"

"Probably a prank call. We don't get deaths around here. At least not outside of the old people's home."

"Well, I need to check it out," Flynn growled, conscious of the fact that a young woman was out there, freaking out about finding a corpse on her morning run. "Are you coming?"

With a derisive snort, he lumbered into the passenger seat. "This better be legit. If you've got me out of my sickbed for a bloody prank call, it'll be you for the morgue."

Flynn started the engine, choosing not to think about the fact that his superior had essentially just asked him to hope for someone's death.

Chapter Nine

Lily remained a few metres from the body. Maybe she should be trying to resuscitate him, but her instincts told her it was too late for that. Perhaps she should walk up to the lane and await PC Grainger, but another instinct made her reluctant to leave Vinny alone.

Her eyes fixed on a rock pool to her left where a small fish darted around, oblivious to the tragedy which had occurred so close to it. She glanced around several times, on the lookout for the police, but when they arrived they did so with such stealth that she only noticed the large, older police officer when he crouched beside Vinny. His voice seemed to drift straight out to sea and she couldn't make out the words, nor whether they were directed at her.

The fish caught her eye again and she fixed her gaze on it until it darted under a rock. Pressure on her shoulder made her flinch dramatically and she whipped around to find PC Grainger beside her.

"Sorry," he said. "Are you okay?"

"Yes." Speaking drew attention to the incessant chattering of her teeth, but she couldn't do anything to stop the tremors in her jaw. "I didn't touch him. Maybe I should have. Should I have done something? CPR or..." She trailed off, unsure what else she might have done and aware of the fact that it made little difference now.

"It's okay," he said. "You did the right thing." His piercing blue eyes held her gaze for a moment before the shout from his colleague drew his attention.

The older man gave a subtle shake of his head. Coupled with his grave expression, it was clear the information he was conveying.

Vinny was definitely dead then. Having it confirmed set Lily's teeth chattering even more violently. She wrapped her arms around herself as her whole body shivered.

"Looks as though he fell," the older police officer said as he took a few steps towards them and pointed at the enormous boulder looming close by. "Poor bugger." His eyes landed on Lily. "I'm sorry," he said sympathetically.

"I don't know him," she said, her words garbled on her shaky voice. "I mean I'm not with him... not friends with him. He's staying at the B&B so I met him. His name's Vinny. That's all I really know. He's a photographer." She stopped, realising she was waffling, providing information that no one had asked for. "I was out for a jog and just saw him there."

"You're staying at the Miller's place?" he asked.

"Yes."

"Do you know if he has family or friends with him?"

She shook her head. "He's with colleagues. They're here on a job together."

"Take her up to the house and see that she gets a warm drink," he said to PC Grainger, who remained solidly by her side. "Take a statement if she's up to it. You'll need to break the news to..." He sighed as his gaze shifted over Lily's shoulder. "Or maybe not."

Following his gaze, Lily spotted the small crowd which had gathered up on the lane beside the police car and an ambulance which had just pulled up. The Millers stood with

Marc and Alanna. A couple of medics spoke to Rodney before setting off across the beach.

"Come on," PC Grainger said, close to Lily's ear. "Let's get you back to the house."

She flicked her eyes back to Vinny, only moving when PC Grainger gently tugged her elbow.

"Watch your footing," he said, drawing her attention to the damp rocks, littered with seaweed. His sturdy black boot landed on a dark green clump – the kind with air pockets, which set off a stutter of popping sounds. She didn't know the names of any type of seaweed, it occurred to her. Maybe she'd look it up later.

"Are you cold?" Flynn asked, his bulk close beside her.

"I don't think so." She wished her teeth would stop chattering so her voice sounded normal. "I just can't stop shivering."

"You had a shock," he said.

The sound of coughing made her turn back, thinking for a moment they'd been wrong about Vinny, and he was now spluttering back to life and possibly gearing up to have another go at someone.

It was just the other police officer, sounding as though he might cough up a lung.

"Don't you get used to seeing dead bodies?" she asked, then blinked in surprise as PC Grainger draped his big black coat around her. She hadn't noticed him removing it, but the warmth was immediately comforting.

"Sadly, yeah." He glanced over at his colleague. "Sergeant Proctor has the flu. He's supposed to be off sick today, but I had to call him in. I've never been so thankful that this wasn't a prank call. If I'd have got him out of bed for something that wasn't life and death, I'd have never heard the end of it."

Lily stared at him, waiting for him to register what he'd said. When he didn't comment further a smile pulled at her lips, and the tremor in her voice had gone when she spoke again. "Did you just say you were happy about the dead body?"

"No." He cast her a rueful glance. "I'm only happy it's not my dead body being dealt with today." He tipped his chin in greeting as the medics passed them, then indicated for Lily to continue with him.

"I take it you're not a fan of Sergeant Proctor?" she asked.

"Other way around... he's not a fan of mine. Give him a reason to have a go at me and he's a happy man."

The openness of the conversation put Lily at ease. Perhaps he wasn't being as professional as the situation warranted, but Lily was glad of it. A normal conversation kept her mind from the dead body behind them.

"How many police are on the islands?" she asked.

"Three now, though it's usually only two. The sergeant and a PC. This is only a temporary position for me."

"Right." She thought of the rumour Seren had shared in the pub. Curious, she opened her mouth to ask why it was a temporary position, but her foot hit a slippery rock and talking shifted down her list of priorities. Instinct sent her arm shooting out and she had the brief thought that taking PC Grainger down with her wouldn't make the situation better. Except his arm was solid when her fingers wrapped around it, and he leaned in to support her with no effort at all. "Thanks," she murmured, annoyed that she'd turned into such a stuttering, jelly-legged liability. "I'm not usually so easily shaken. Though I guess I don't stumble across dead bodies very often."

Her mind took her back to the last time she'd encountered a dead body. Finding her uncle had been a devastating experience, but one she thought she'd dealt with well. With hindsight, she wondered if refusing to think about it was as clever a tactic as she'd thought.

With a long stride, PC Grainger stepped from the rocks to the sand, then held a hand out to help her.

"What on earth has happened?" Mrs Miller asked, approaching them.

Alanna crowded in too. "Is that Vinny out there?"

"Yes," Lily replied, automatically looking back to where the medics were now deep in conversation with the sergeant.

"Is he okay?" Alanna's eyes were wide.

"I'm afraid not," PC Grainger said, his voice soft and full of sympathy.

Chapter Ten

"Dead?" Alanna muttered for about the fiftieth time. She sat on the couch with Marc, while Lily felt dwarfed by the large armchair beside the patio doors.

After fielding questions from the group as best he could, PC Grainger had ushered them all back to the house where they'd settled in the living room. The whole thing felt like a blur to Lily and she couldn't even guess at how much time had passed since she'd found Vinny. She'd stuck by PC Grainger, moving when he moved and not paying too much attention to the surrounding chatter. As she lifted her gaze, she caught him looking down at her. His eyes darted away and he accepted a steaming mug from Mrs Miller with a puzzled expression. Immediately, she took it from him again with a shake of the head.

"You said you didn't want anything," Flora murmured. "This was for Lily."

"I'm also fine," Lily said.

"You've had a shock." There was a tremble to Mrs Miller's hand as she gave Lily the mug. "Sweet tea. That's what you need. Drink up."

"How can he be dead?" Alanna screeched, looking accusingly at PC Grainger.

"That fog." Mr Miller kept his head low as he loitered just inside the doorway with Oscar beside him. "It was so thick this morning, I'll bet he didn't even see the edge of the rock. Probably just stumbled right off the edge."

Alanna let out a strangled cry. "But he's so young. He just turned thirty. He can't be dead. He can't."

"I'm sorry," PC Grainger said. "Did any of you see him this morning? It's good if we can put together a timeline of his movements."

"I um..." Oscar's voice was a low whisper from the side of the room but it got everyone's attention. "I saw him going out when I arrived for work," he said. "That would have been around nine."

Beside him, Mr Miller nodded. "Yes, I saw him then, too. I said good morning to him and mentioned the terrible weather, but he wasn't chatty. He walked out of the door as Oscar came in. Then I went to help Flora in the kitchen."

At the mention of her name, Mrs Miller seemed to snap to attention. "Oh," she said. "I didn't see Vinny at all, but I heard Oscar arrive at nine. He came into the kitchen to say hello before he went out to do some work in the garden." She nodded, as though recalling the events in her mind. "Rodney came in at the same time as him." She smiled at her husband.

"Did he mention to anyone what his plan was for the morning?" PC Grainger asked.

Oscar shook his head, as did Mr Miller.

"We wanted to get the ferry this morning," Alanna said. "We all wanted to get home. Vinny was upset about his camera and was keen to leave. But when I looked up the time for the ferry, I found it wasn't running today because of the fog. He was annoyed about that, wasn't he?" She turned to Marc, who'd been rubbing circles on her back while she spoke.

Lily blew on the mug of tea in her hands before taking a sip. She winced at the excessive sweetness.

"He was a little agitated," Marc said.

"He said if we had to stay longer we should at least look for different accommodation." Alanna looked at Mrs Miller. "Sorry, but he didn't like it here, and after the business with his camera he was very upset."

"Okay." PC Grainger appeared to be taking notes without ever looking down at his pen and paper. "Do you know what his immediate plan was when he left here?"

Alanna looked at Marc with panic-filled eyes. "He said he needed fresh air. Oh, god, I argued with him. I can't believe I argued with him and now he's dead." She lifted her ball of soggy tissues to her face as another sob erupted.

"I know this is difficult," PC Grainger said softly. "But anything you can remember could be helpful. Did you argue with him this morning?"

"No." She blew her nose. "Last week, wasn't it?" Once again, she looked at her boyfriend as though needing his clarification on events. When he smiled gently, she nodded and turned back to PC Grainger. "Last week. We had a disagreement and I suggested we shouldn't work together any more."

"But you've been working together since then?" PC Grainger asked. "Working on your blog? Do I have that right? He takes the photographs?"

"Yes. We argued and then we just carried on as though it hadn't happened." She reached for Marc's hand. "I feel terrible now. You told me I was being too harsh on him. You were right." She smiled sadly. "Is he really dead?"

Marc didn't reply, just swiped a tear from her cheek with his thumb. A delicate gesture for such a well-built guy.

A loud crackling tore through the air before a voice came over PC Grainger's walkie-talkie. "Sorry," he said, moving it to his ear as he wandered out of the room.

"I just can't believe it," Alanna cried again.

Mrs Miller joined her on the couch and gave her arm a gentle pat. "It's a shock," she said tearfully. "Such a shock. I can't get my head around it myself."

Their chatter made it impossible for Lily to hear what PC Grainger was saying out in the hallway, but she concentrated on the cadence of his voice regardless.

When he returned, he directed his attention at Alanna. "Sorry to keep asking you questions, but I wonder if you know who we should contact... family members or a next of kin?"

"Oh, goodness." She bit down on her lip as she looked at Marc. "There was just his sister, wasn't there?" Without waiting for Marc's input, she returned her attention to PC Grainger. "His parents died when he was a teenager. He spent a few years living with his grandma after that, but she's dead now too. So there's just Rachel, his sister. They weren't close but she'd surely want to know." She clutched at Marc's hand. "She'd want to know, wouldn't she?"

"She should be told," Marc said. "I can't think of anyone else off the top of my head. He spent most of his time with us these days. We travelled a lot in the last few years. Since Alanna's blog took off."

"Yes." Alanna dabbed at more tears which spilled down her cheeks. "I guess we were like family to him."

"Could you give me his sister's full name?" PC Grainger asked.

"Yes." Alanna reached for her phone which hung by her side in a clear pouch attached to a gold chain. "I can give you her phone number too. We used to hang out sometimes. Back before she and Vinny fell out. And before I got famous," she added with a measure of pride that made Lily sip at her tea to hide her amusement.

While PC Grainger took the details from Alanna, Lily's gaze shifted to Oscar who tapped rapidly on his phone. She supposed this was quite exciting for a teenager living on a small island. For any teenager, for that matter, but it must be really shocking around here. She imagined him sharing the details with his friends like it was a juicy piece of gossip.

"Should I get on with some work or something?" he said, his head flicking up abruptly.

"Oh, no." Mrs Miller shook her head. "Don't worry about working today, love. There's nothing urgent, anyway."

"I don't mind," he said, looking suddenly desperate to escape the room. "I can go out and get on with the garden work. Unless you need to ask me anything," he said to PC Grainger, who shook his head.

"I don't want you working," Mrs Miller said, eyes filling with tears. "It feels wrong somehow, to just carry on as though nothing has happened."

"Can I go home then?" he asked uncertainly.

"Yes," Mrs Miller said. "You get home if you want to."

"Actually," PC Grainger said. "If you could just hang on for a bit."

"Why?" Alanna screeched. "We're not suspects or anything, are we? You said it was an accident."

"You're all free to leave whenever you like," PC Grainger said calmly. "It's only that they're about to move the body. You might prefer not to see." He shot a sympathetic glance at Oscar who swallowed hard.

"I'll wait a bit," he mumbled.

Beside him, Mr Miller rubbed a hand frantically across his forehead. "What an absolute nightmare. I can't believe it."

Lily wondered how many times that statement had been uttered in the last hour. Disbelief was apparently the sentiment of the day.

Another crackling voice came loudly but unintelligibly over the walkie-talkie and PC Grainger retreated to the hallway again.

"This is going to be bad for business," Mr Miller muttered, shaking his head.

"Rodney!" his wife spat. "What a thing to say."

"Sorry." He looked apologetically at Alanna. "That was insensitive. Ignore me. It's just the shock of it. My head is all over the place."

"No," Alanna said, her tears seeming to evaporate. "You're right. This is terrible. Oh, my goodness." She slapped a hand over her chest. "What if Vinny was right?"

"What are you talking about?" Marc asked gently.

Alanna looked at him with a horrified expression. "He said that his photographs were the cornerstone of my blog. That without him, I'd be nothing. What if he was right?"

"I don't think that's something you need to worry about." Marc tucked a lock of her hair behind her ear only for it to fall immediately forward again.

"No," Mrs Miller agreed soothingly. "Besides, I'm sure your followers will be very sympathetic, given the circumstances."

Alanna's hand went to her mouth and she sat up straighter. "Yes. They should be sympathetic to my grief. I'll write a post about what happened. A nice tribute to him. They'll all be sympathetic. Maybe I'll even get more followers from it," she ventured.

"Maybe." Mrs Miller patted her hand.

"I won't write about it today," Alanna said decisively. "That would be insensitive. Maybe tomorrow, or the day after."

PC Grainger slipped back into the room while Alanna continued to debate the best time to post on social media. He went straight over to Lily.

"Are you okay?" he asked.

"Yes." She had the full mug of tea in her hand and nowhere to put it. "I can't drink it," she whispered. "It's more sugar than tea."

Taking it from her, he set it on the coffee table then returned and crouched beside her chair. "How are you feeling? You had quite a shock."

"I'm okay. It feels a little surreal."

"That's normal."

"Do I need to hang around here?"

"No."

She nodded, then pondered what else she would do. Going up and sitting alone in her room wasn't overly appealing. Going out also felt inappropriate.

"I don't know what to do," she said.

"Stay here, then," he said. "You're probably better being around other people."

"Yes." She nodded. Being with other people was a good plan.

He cleared his throat. "Since you found him, we'll need you to make a statement."

"Oh, okay." She met his gaze. "How does that work?"

"You can just write down everything you remember. Or, if you'd rather, you can go over everything with me and I can write it for you."

"Yes, please. Let's do that."

He nodded. "Let's find somewhere private and you can tell me now while it's fresh in your mind."

She sucked in a breath, uncomfortable at the idea of reliving the discovery, but also relieved by the thought of getting away from Alanna's inappropriate chatter about her blog and how best to break the news to her followers.

Chapter Eleven

AFTER THE TENSION in the living room, the quiet in the breakfast room was welcome. PC Grainger gently guided Lily through her recollection of the morning and finding Vinny's body. It was pretty straightforward, and he didn't even seem to make many notes as she spoke. Once she'd finished talking, she let out a breath of relief.

"Are you okay?" he asked with a smile.

"Yes. I think so."

"Would you like a drink that isn't laced with sugar?"

"Please. Coffee would be good."

He went to the table at the side of the room and made drinks for them both before coming back to sit with her.

"What will happen now?" she asked, wrapping her hands around the warm mug.

"I'll write it up later, then I'll just need you to read over it and sign it if everything is correct."

"Right." She hadn't meant about the statement. "But what happens with everything else?"

His lips pulled to one side. "Do you mean with the body? Arrangements will be made to have him taken back to the mainland."

She gave a low hum of acknowledgement, but that also wasn't the answer she was looking for. "Will there be an autopsy?" she asked. "And an investigation?"

Slowly, he shook his head. "That would only happen if there were suspicious circumstances."

"How do you decide if circumstances are suspicious?" She leaned forward, resting her elbows on the table.

PC Grainger leaned back in his seat. "I suppose if there is anything which seems off. If we had any reason to believe it wasn't an accident..."

"But there's nothing like that with Vinny?"

His left eyebrow quirked upwards. "It doesn't seem so. If the sergeant thought it was anything other than an accident, the body wouldn't have been removed so quickly."

Lily pursed her lips. "But how could he really tell? And doesn't he need to speak to people as well?"

"Like who?"

Lily tipped her head toward the voices from the living room.

"I spoke to them," PC Grainger pointed out.

"Did you tell Sergeant Proctor about it?"

"I gave him the highlights. Is there something in particular you think I should have told him?"

Lily shrugged. "Alanna had recently argued with him," she said. "Mr Miller had also been unhappy with him. You saw them arguing yesterday?"

His lips barely shifted, but his amusement was clear in the sparkle in his eyes. He leaned forwards and whispered. "Are you suggesting Mr Miller killed him because he complained about burnt bacon?"

"No." Lily's lips pulled into a wide smile and the accompanying warmth in her belly felt like a relief after the sombre morning. "Sorry," she said, realising how she must sound. "I only really wondered what the procedure was. My imagination might have flipped into overdrive for a moment."

His smile was warm and friendly. "It's my experience that when something looks like an accident, nine times out of ten, that's exactly what it is."

She nodded, feeling silly.

"Sorry to interrupt," Mrs Miller said, appearing in the doorway. "How are you getting on in here?"

"We're all done," PC Grainger said.

"Great." She opened the door wider. "I just realised no one has had breakfast. I don't suppose anyone really feels like a proper meal, but I thought I could get some bacon sandwiches going." She made her way across the room. "You'd both eat one, wouldn't you?"

They nodded and she continued into the kitchen. Lily wondered if PC Grainger was also thinking about their previous conversation.

She was biting back a grin when he leaned in. "She better not burn the bacon," he whispered. "I can't be held responsible for my actions if she does."

Lily covered her mouth as a laugh escaped her. Her eyes widened and she tried to reprimand him with a stern look. "You can't say that!"

"Sorry," he said, not looking remotely remorseful. "Copper's humour. You have to find ways to make light of stuff or you go crazy."

"It's a little inappropriate, though."

One corner of his mouth twitched. "You started it by suggesting Mr Miller had committed murder over burnt bacon."

"Over a bad review, actually," she said. "But I see your point."

When he said it back to her, it did sound fairly absurd.

Chapter Twelve

FOR THE FIRST time since he'd arrived on the island, Flynn's day didn't drag at all. It was something he missed about his old life – being so busy that time slipped by without notice.

He spent the entire morning at the Miller's place, piecing together Vinny's final movements while also attempting to keep everyone calm. Lily had been the easiest on that score. Once she got over the shock of finding the body, she seemed to take it all in her stride. Or perhaps it was the contrast with Alanna's hysterics which made Lily seem so cool.

Back at the station, he wrote up his report, and Lily's statement, while his ears pricked up frequently to listen in on Sergeant Proctor's phone calls. That seemed to be the most effective way for him to keep abreast of everything to do with today's incident. He'd tried the more traditional approach of speaking to his superior, but that mostly felt like conversing with a moody teenager.

"Couldn't have been worse timing," Sergeant Proctor muttered following a particularly drawn-out coughing fit. It had occurred to PC Grainger a couple of times to suggest the sergeant went back home to bed, but he imagined it wouldn't be a welcome suggestion – not coming from Flynn, anyway – so he held his tongue.

"Excuse me?" Flynn asked, noticing the sergeant was looking at him expectantly. He hadn't even registered that the words were directed at him.

"I said it's terrible timing." He paused and Flynn pondered how to respond. Being spoken to by Sergeant Proctor without him barking orders at him was something of a novelty. "What with PC Hill off ill. I could've done with him around today."

"Is there something else you'd like me to do?" Flynn offered.

"No," the sergeant snapped. "There's also not a lot we can do at the moment. We can't move the body off the island until this weather clears, and it's looking as though the fog might hang around for a day or two." He erupted into another coughing fit, and Flynn noticed the sheen of sweat across his forehead. Again, he refrained from suggesting he go home to bed.

After a moment, Sergeant Proctor caught his breath and looked resignedly at Flynn. "I suppose you can hold the fort here if I go home for a while."

"Of course," Flynn said, hiding his positivity at the notion. "I've written up my report and the statement for Miss Larkin."

Sergeant Proctor walked over to Flynn's desk and frowned in obvious confusion.

"The woman who found the body," Flynn clarified.

"Ah, yes. Of course."

"I'll go over and get her signature on it tomorrow. Is there anything else you want me to deal with? A press release maybe?" He winced, wondering if that was even something they bothered about on the islands. Was the press even interested?

"I already did it," Sergeant Proctor said. "And I have all the relevant people on standby for moving the body to the mainland as soon as the weather permits. I'll try to keep any press interest at bay until we've informed the next of kin, though." He dropped a piece of paper in front of Flynn with a name and phone number on it. "That's the details of the deceased's sister. I tried calling twice but got no answer. Keep trying her." He let out a long breath. "You have dealt with this sort of thing before, I take it? You can be sensitive when breaking the news?"

"Yes," Flynn said, gritting his teeth to keep from saying any more. Like pointing out that he was twenty-seven and not actually a child. That he'd been in the force for nine years and had routinely dealt with similar situations. And mostly to shout at him that he wasn't completely incompetent and that their time together would be much more pleasant if he'd stop treating him as though he was.

He smiled benignly and reached for the piece of paper. "I can manage that."

"If anything else comes up, call me." Sergeant Proctor was already walking away. "Anything," he growled. "Don't go making decisions without running them by me."

"Yes, Sarge," Flynn said brightly, deciding to focus on the positive – he had the place to himself for the rest of the afternoon.

Not that he liked to wish illness on anyone, but he couldn't help but hope it might take the sergeant a few more days to fully recover.

Chapter Thirteen

THERE WAS something about PC Grainger's presence that made Lily feel anchored. While he was there, she felt safe and comfortable. Once he left she felt out of place around the Millers and Alanna and Marc. Possibly because she was aware of the fact that she'd insinuated to PC Grainger that one of them may be a murderer.

She spent the afternoon lying on her bed, staring at the ceiling and listening to the noises in the house. Eventually, she heard the doorbell and then the back and forth of a conversation before the creak of the stairs told her someone was coming up. The gentle knock on her door surprised her, and she stared at it for a moment before she moved.

Had it really only been twenty-four hours ago that Vinny had been pummelling on the door and demanding entrance? No one was demanding anything now, though. In fact, the knock had been so light that she wasn't even certain it was someone at her door until she opened it.

The barmaid from the pub looked at her sympathetically. "I hope I'm not intruding," she said, words dripping with apology. "I heard what happened... that some guy staying here had died, and I knew you were staying here, so I wanted to check on you. Flora just told me you were the one who found him." She tilted her head. "Are you okay?"

"I think so. It's been a very weird day."

Seren gave a half smile. "It must have been awful."

Instinctively, Lily wanted to say it hadn't been so bad, but an image of Vinny's twisted body came back to her and she swallowed hard. "Yeah," she murmured. "It was pretty awful."

"I have a shift at the pub tonight," Seren told her. "If you want company, you could come and prop up the bar again. Kit will probably come in at some point too."

"Thank you." Lily considered the idea. "I actually don't feel like going out." She screwed her face up as a thought occurred to her. "Except I don't have any food here, so I suppose I'll need to go out at some point." Maybe, under the circumstances, Mrs Miller might cook something for her. She could at least ask.

"Oh!" Seren's eyes lit up. "I almost forgot... I brought you crab cakes. They're my favourite comfort food and I thought you might need something comforting." She looked suddenly uncertain. "I don't even know if you like crab cakes, but if you do these are probably the best you've ever tasted. There are chips too." Reaching into the bag in her hand, she retrieved a takeaway box and handed it over.

"Thanks so much." Lily took it eagerly, only now realising how hungry she was. "That's really kind of you."

"I bought some for myself as well," Seren said. "We can eat together if you want, or if you'd rather be alone, I'll leave you in peace."

Lily was happy to have company and opened the door wider before she frowned at the space she was inviting Seren into – a bedroom. "We could eat downstairs if you want..."

"No, let's eat in here." Seren moved inside. "Flora's downstairs. She'd probably sit with us and we won't be able to talk properly."

Lily felt the same sense of ease that she'd felt with PC

Grainger as she watched Seren settle herself in the armchair with her takeaway box on her lap.

Out of the blue, Lily heard her uncle's voice ringing in her ear. *Don't get too attached,* it said with Uncle Derek's kindly tone. *You know we won't be staying long.*

In her mind's eye, she could see him ruffling her hair as he said the words. And he'd promise to buy her a treat in the next city or town they moved to – often in an entirely different country. As though a new toy would make up for not having friends.

Her breath stopped as she was suddenly deep in a recollection of the arguments they'd had when she'd finally tired of being dragged from one place to the next. And then the last words she'd spoken to him... telling him he'd ruined her life. She'd wanted to take them back immediately, but her stubborn streak had made her wait a day before going to apologise.

He'd been dead when she'd whispered her apology in his ear, while squeezing his cold, lifeless hand.

"Oh, my goodness." Seren removed her takeaway box from her lap and set it aside. "I'm so sorry. I'm like the most insensitive person ever. I just waltzed in and started stuffing my face. Are you okay? We can talk if you want. I just thought you might prefer to eat before we get to the subject of the dead body..."

Snapped from her memories, Lily realised she was still standing by the open door. She wasn't in floods of tears, so that was something. Still, she must look like she'd lost the plot. She forced her muscles to relax as she closed the door.

"It's fine," she said. "I'm starving. I just zoned out for a moment there."

"You've got a lot on your mind," Seren said. "Eat up and then you can tell me all about it. Maybe it will help to get it off your chest."

Lily sat at the dressing table to eat and didn't bother to

wait until she'd finished to give Seren the details of her morning.

"It's frightening, isn't it?" Seren said. "Thinking that life can come to an end so quickly. It gives me the willies just thinking about it."

Lily pushed her empty takeaway box aside. "PC Grainger was great," she said, knowing Seren would be interested in that bit of info. Also, she wanted to correct Seren's view of him being grumpy and rude. Lily hadn't seen that at all. "Really calm and kind," she said.

"That's good," Seren said softly.

Lily nodded. "They say it was an accident."

"The rocks get slippery," Seren said. "And the fog is intense today. You can barely see your hand in front of your face."

"They don't do any kind of investigation though," Lily mused. "That surprised me."

Seren was about to pop a chip in her mouth, but stopped abruptly and set it back in the box on her lap before closing the lid. "What's really hard with situations like this," she said with a gravity to her tone that took Lily by surprise, "is not knowing exactly what happened. His family will never know precisely how he came to fall. That kind of stuff can haunt you."

"Are you speaking from experience?" Lily probed.

The way Seren shook her head made it seem as though she might brush the conversation aside, but after a small hesitation she kept talking. "Kit's dad died in a boating accident," she said. "He was on his own, so we'll never know exactly what happened. It's hard for Kit and his family."

"And you?" Lily ventured, recognising the grief in Seren's eyes.

"Kit's dad was great," she said, an air of melancholy to her words. A moment later, she smiled gently. "Sorry. I wanted to check you were okay, not make you more depressed." She sat up straighter. "Let's lighten the atmosphere... you said PC

Grainger was calm and kind, but I'd also like to know if he was flirting with you today."

That definitely changed the atmosphere and the laughter that bubbled out of Lily felt wonderful.

Don't get too attached, the voice in her head chimed again, but she shoved it to one side. She was only staying on the island for a week, so she wasn't in a position to be making lasting friendships, regardless of how much she longed to.

But right at that moment she felt she had a friend, on a day when she really needed one.

"Did he flirt?" Seren demanded. "He totally did, didn't he?"

"No." Lily tried to keep a straight face but couldn't manage it. "He was completely professional."

"Well, you need to watch out, because he's probably going to try and sleep with you."

Lily shook her head defiantly.

"I bet you he will." Seren let out a dramatic gasp. "You don't even care, do you? Do you have a thing for PC Grainger?"

"No!" Lily suspected there was no way Seren would believe her unless she could stop with her incessant grinning.

But no matter how hard she tried, she couldn't shift her features to anything resembling a serious expression, and the more she denied any romantic feeling towards PC Grainger, the less Seren seemed to believe her.

Chapter Fourteen

MONDAY

THE DOOR to the station was propped open with a wooden wedge. Peeking inside, all Lily could see was a wall of cupboards and a polished desk with a wooden chair behind it. Leaning to look further into the room, a second desk came into view and the weary features of PC Grainger. With one hand he held a phone against his ear while the other hand massaged his temple. The conversation revolved around the weather so Lily felt no guilt over eavesdropping. It seemed to be the tail end of a conversation, anyway.

He ended the call and let out a low groan as he leaned far back in his chair, putting him outside of Lily's vision. She rapped on the solid wood door as she stepped inside.

"Hi," she said, sending PC Grainger springing to an upright position. His black shirt complemented his olive skin and Lily felt her cheeks heat as she recalled her conversation with Seren yesterday.

"Miss Larkin." PC Grainger cleared his throat. "How are you today?"

Being called Miss Larkin cooled her thoughts down again pretty quickly.

"Lily," she mumbled, hating formalities at the best of times, but also feeling they were beyond formalities after their shared experience yesterday. Except, it wasn't really a shared experience. He'd been doing his job. The fact that he'd made her feel so at ease merely showed how good he was at his job. "I'm fine," she told him, as she crossed the room. Her gaze drifted to a stack of papers beside him, held down by a black walkie-talkie. When her eyes strayed back to PC Grainger, he gave her a questioning half smile.

"I'm not sure what to do with myself," she said to fill the silence.

"You had a shock yesterday." He tipped his chin at the chair opposite him. "It'll take time to process it."

Nodding, she lowered herself into the chair. "Do you need to ask me any more questions or anything?"

"No, but you could read over your statement. I'd intended to bring it over to the bed and breakfast later." Moving the walkie-talkie aside, he thumbed through the papers, then passed a single A4 sheet to Lily. "Have a read through it and make sure everything is correct. Take your time."

He switched his attention to his computer screen, giving Lily space to read. Her eyes scanned the words with an odd feeling of detachment. It was as though the events of the previous day had been told by someone else and not by her. She was nearing the end of the page when the walkie-talkie crackled to life, the sudden sound startling her.

PC Grainger tilted his head, listening to the voice which was mostly garbled to Lily's ears.

"Sorry," he said, catching her eye as the room fell silent again. Barely a moment passed before more chatter broke the silence. "I can just..." PC Grainger trailed off as he turned a knob until it clicked and plunged them back into quiet. Lily tried to focus on the words on the page.

"Don't you need to respond or something?" she asked when curiosity got the better of her.

He shook his head. "It wasn't anything to do with me."

"How does that work, then?" Lily set the paper on the desk.

PC Grainger blew out a breath. "This police station belongs to Devon and Cornwall Police. We're all on the same frequency."

"So you can hear what everyone else is called out to?"

He nodded once.

"Are you supposed to just turn it off?" She eyed the walkie-talkie dubiously.

"It's fine. If we get called out, I'd switch it on to keep in touch with dispatch, but most of the time we're just listening in on what's going on over on the mainland."

"But if there's an emergency here, how do you find out about it?"

"It's rare for there to be a 999 call from the islands. If there is, and the dispatchers can't get us on the radio, they call the station or one of our mobiles, but as I say, it's rare. If anyone has an issue around here, they mostly just wander in and tell us." He rolled his eyes. "Or they tag us on social media."

Assuming it was a joke, Lily laughed, then stopped when she caught the earnest set of his features. "You're not serious?"

"I'm very serious."

"How can that be efficient? I can't imagine getting burgled and deciding to hop on social media to report it instead of making a phone call."

Now it was his turn to laugh, and the sound made Lily smile despite missing the joke. "What's funny?" she asked.

"Nothing. You just overestimated the level of crime on the islands. There are no burglaries. If someone's reporting something, it's along the lines of littering, or inconveniently parked golf buggies, maybe a misplaced bike here and there. There's nothing as exciting as burglaries. There's no real crime around here."

"You say that, but yesterday we were standing beside a dead body."

He raised an eyebrow. "Last I heard, slipping and falling wasn't a crime."

Lily dropped her gaze back to the statement in her hands and let her eyes sweep over the final few sentences. "This all seems correct," she said after a moment.

"Good. I'll just need your signature on it." He nudged a pen across the desk.

She picked up the pen, then hesitated. "I was thinking about something..."

"If you need me to change anything, I can do that. It's not a problem."

Lily was momentarily confused, until she saw him glance at the paper in front of her.

"Oh, no. There's nothing wrong with the statement. I was only thinking earlier about his camera. Vinny's camera. The one that was lost or stolen or whatever."

"What about it?"

"I just..." She tipped her head to one side. "Don't you think it's odd that he had his camera stolen and then the next day..." Okay, when she said it out loud, it seemed a bit of a leap to think the two things were connected. Instead of finishing her statement, she tapped the pen on the desk.

"There really isn't anything to indicate that what happened was anything other than a tragic accident." He ran a hand over his jaw, drawing attention to his dark stubble. "It seems that Mr Roth had a run of bad luck."

"*Bad luck?*" Lily covered her mouth with her hand to disguise her involuntary snort. "The guy's dead."

PC Grainger scrubbed his hands over his face. "Sorry.

Poor choice of words." His eyes went to the paper on the desk. "Are you sure there isn't anything you'd like to amend or add?"

"No." Quietly, she scribbled her name, then pushed the paper across the desk.

"If you think of anything else, feel free to get in touch."

"Thanks." She moved on autopilot to the door, saying a curt goodbye as she left.

Chapter Fifteen

THE EVENTS of the past twenty-four hours had kept Lily's thoughts firmly away from the reason for her trip to St. Mary's. Something which seemed like quite the feat considering how much the photograph of the ice cream shop had consumed her in the past months.

It only came back to her when she passed the solicitor's office while wandering back through Hugh Town after leaving the police station.

Without a lot of thought, she pressed the doorbell and was surprised by a loud buzzing sound a moment later. The door opened with a click when she pushed it. Stepping inside, she glanced around the barren hallway with bright white walls. A door to her left opened and a tall, wiry man appeared and squinted over his reading glasses.

"Can I help you?" he asked with a blank look.

"Maybe. I'm not sure. Are you Paul Greaves?"

"Yes."

"The solicitor?"

He eyed her warily. "Yes. You're not local, are you?"

"No." She shifted her weight. "I wondered if I could ask

Hannah Ellis

you a few questions about the property near Porthcressa Beach that was once an ice cream shop."

He rolled his eyes dramatically. "Did Kit Treneary send you? Because I can only tell you what I've told him many times – it's not for sale."

"I don't want to buy it," she said quickly. "I'm only interested in..." Her brain stuttered. What *was* she interested in? Why had she got so obsessed with an old photo and a flicker of a memory?

"I'm just interested in knowing more about the building and the owner," she finally said, with a surge of confidence that came from knowing that she wouldn't be satisfied until she found out everything she could. Eagerly, she dived into her bag and took out the photograph. "I remember visiting the ice cream shop when I was young," she told Mr Greaves. "I recently found this photo and spent quite some time tracking the place down. If you could spare five minutes to talk to me, I'd appreciate it."

He blew out a breath and retreated into the room, leaving the door open in what Lily assumed was as an invitation to follow.

"Thank you so much," she said trailing after him. "I promise I won't keep you long."

The room contained a large desk and a leather office chair. Two more chairs were placed at the other side of the desk, and a sideboard held tea and coffee making equipment. Taking a seat opposite Mr Greaves, Lily's eyes roamed the wall of bookcases behind him before settling on his expectant features.

"I'm afraid there isn't much I can tell you about the building," he said. "It closed down around twenty years ago."

"Because of a fire?" Lily asked.

He removed his glasses. "There was a fire, but it was only minor. As far as I'm aware it wasn't the reason for the closing."

"What *was* the reason?"

"The owner moved back to the mainland."

"Just out of the blue?" She frowned. "Why would they move away and not do anything with the building? Given its location, I assume it's worth something, and I know there's a demand for the property because Kit told me he'd been trying to buy it."

"So you *do* know Kit?"

"Not really. I bumped into him and we got chatting about the ice cream shop. Anyway, why didn't the owner sell it when they left the island?"

He shrugged. "I suppose they wanted to hang onto it."

"*They* as in *owners* plural? Or did you mean *they* in the non-binary sense, or are you being deliberately obtuse?"

"The latter," he said dryly.

"It's a woman though, right? The owner is the same person who owned and ran the shop twenty years ago?" In Lily's memory it had been a woman who'd shown her the ice cream machines, and she was convinced she'd been the owner.

He nodded slowly.

"So the owner is a she. Why has she never sold the place?"

"Because she wanted to keep it, I suppose."

"You suppose?" she asked, exasperated by his lack of openness.

He shrugged again. "I don't ask a lot of questions. That's not part of my job."

"What is your job?"

"Legal advice for the owner." He hesitated. "I also have power of attorney over the building."

"Does that mean you could sell it?"

"No." He rubbed the bridge of his nose. "I can't make decisions like that. If there's any kind of tax issue, or local council concerns... something of that nature, I'm authorised to deal with it."

"Council concerns?" Lily asked.

"Complaints about the building being an eyesore, that sort of thing..."

"Have people complained?"

"There was some discussion around it," he said blithely. "Around the same time Kit Treneary set his eye on the place, though he swears the complaint didn't come from him."

Lily shook her head, realising they'd got off topic. "How long was it an ice cream shop before it closed down?"

His lips pinched together. "I think it would have been around two or three years."

"Not long then," she mused. "Was it profitable?"

The question seemed to take him by surprise and his eyebrows dipped.

"If it wasn't, that would at least explain it closing. It still doesn't shed any light on why the building wasn't sold."

Mr Greaves leaned on the desk, steepling his fingers in front of his chin. "Is there a reason for all your questions?"

"I don't actually know," she said truthfully. "I found the photograph and got intrigued." She stared at the photo in her hands, annoyed with herself for getting so attached to the idea of tracking down the shop. "It's daft," she murmured. "But my parents died shortly after the photo was taken. I only discovered the picture recently and it stirred some memories."

She squeezed her eyes closed, pushing aside the voice in her head that insisted she was looking for some connection that didn't exist. "I had a feeling that my parents knew the owner... that they were friends, maybe. I'm not sure, but would it be possible for you to put me in touch with her so I could ask?" Given that he'd seemed not to even want to reveal the gender of the owner, it seemed unlikely he'd hand over their contact details, but she had to at least ask.

Paul's features softened a little. "I'm sorry. I can't give out the details of my clients, but I can tell you this – the owner of the ice cream shop was friendly and well-liked back when she

84

lived here. There's every chance your memory has mistaken friendly professionalism for a personal connection which didn't exist. I hardly imagine they would remember holiday-makers who visited the shop twenty years ago."

Lily sighed. "You're probably right."

"I'm sorry I can't be more helpful," he said, standing to put an end to their meeting.

"Thank you anyway," she said. "If you speak to the owner, maybe you could mention my name and my parents' names... just ask if they knew my parents."

"I really don't think..."

Clinging to the idea, Lily reached across the desk for the notepad and a pen. "I can jot the names down, and my number." She scribbled away. "I'll be on the island until Friday. Over at the Miller's bed and breakfast. After that, I'll be back home in Truro."

She winced at the mention of home. After her uncle had died she'd impulsively returned to her place of birth and rented an apartment. Truro had seemed like a convenient base to conduct her search from. She wasn't quite convinced her pokey flat with her few belongings was worthy of the title 'home', but never mind.

"You can call me anytime," she told Mr Greaves.

"You're staying at the Miller's?" he asked.

"Yes."

"Terrible business yesterday, with the guy on the rocks. You didn't know him, did you?"

"No. I met him, but I didn't know him."

"It's just awful," Mr Greaves said. "Poor fella." He shook his head as he moved to the door. "This could well be the final nail in Rodney's coffin, too."

"How do you mean?" Lily asked.

"Sorry." He let out a humourless laugh. "That was a poor choice of words. I was only thinking that Rodney keeps saying his wife is only one good reason away from carting him off to live on the mainland. The death of a guest seems like all the argument she needs to get her way."

"I heard she wants to be close to her grandchildren."

Mr Greaves opened the door and gave a small smile. "I suspect she might get her wish now."

Chapter Sixteen

It didn't make sense. That was the thought that Lily kept coming back to as she made her way across the misty island. Why would someone walk away from a business unless it wasn't doing well? And if it wasn't doing well, why not sell the place?

Leaving the ice cream shop abandoned not only seemed like a terrible financial decision, but also an unethical one. The owner would have known how an empty building would look in such a beautiful setting. Whoever had complained about it being an eyesore hadn't been wrong.

She also couldn't understand the element of secrecy around the owner. What would cause their need for anonymity? That also didn't make sense because if it was the same owner, someone must remember them from when they lived and worked on the island.

That notion made Lily's racing thoughts slow down. If the solicitor was unwilling to give her the details of the owner, a better approach was to ask around and find out her name. With her name, Lily could probably track her down herself.

Glancing around, she was surprised to find the B&B in sight.

An eerie silence greeted her when she walked through the front door. Usually there were signs of life, but now it was completely still. She hesitated a moment, expecting Mrs Miller to appear and ask if she needed anything, or Mr Miller popping up to say hello.

No one materialised.

The absence of people felt like an invitation to make herself at home. Instead of going straight upstairs, Lily went into the breakfast room and made a beeline for the coffee machine. With a hot mug in her hand, she wandered to the living room.

The patio door was perfectly silent when she slid it open to step out into the back garden. Birdsong filled the damp air as she sat and sipped her coffee. After a few minutes, a brown sparrow came and hopped around her feet before fluttering away again.

Lily was halfway down her coffee when a noise drew her attention. A crash, as though someone had dropped something. It came again almost immediately. Moving from her chair, she called a questioning 'hello' as she peered around the side of the house to where the garden shed stood beside the border wall.

All was quiet again and she was about to return to her coffee when a jolt of curiosity propelled her towards the shed. Peering through the window wasn't helpful. In the dim light, she couldn't make out much.

Deciding she'd probably imagined the noise, she was all set to turn back when the silence was broken once again. This time it sounded like a tree branch scraping against the shed, except there was no breeze and all the branches were perfectly still.

Slowly, she slid the bolt which fixed the shed door in place. The hinges groaned as she opened the door, then silence consumed the air again.

With tense shoulders, she stepped inside, telling herself there was nothing to fear. Her body didn't get the message and her heart pounded in her rib cage while the tiny hairs on her arms stood on end. She shivered in the shadowy room and almost laughed at herself. There was nothing except for the usual gardening equipment: a lawn mower in the corner, a coiled hose pipe, a bunch of plant pots—

A high-pitched yowl shattered the silence.

Plastic flower pots flew from the shelf and ricocheted off Lily's shoulder.

Instinct had her stumbling backwards, which meant the handle of the spade just missed her feet when it fell to the floor with a clatter.

Lily's heart smashed against her ribcage so hard that it might have left a bruise.

"It's just a cat," she said out loud, in an attempt to calm her frazzled nervous system. "Only a cat. Nothing to be scared of."

The silky tabby had the audacity to hiss at her before darting away.

"I let you out, didn't I?" Lily called after it. "Maybe a thank you would be more appropriate. And an apology for shortening my lifespan wouldn't go amiss either."

With a deep breath, she bent for the handle of the spade and propped it back against the wall. Then she collected up the plant pots, which rolled around her feet. As she went to insert into a space on the shelf, her eyes landed on a leather strap at the back of the shelf. Instinctively, she pulled on the strap, surprised by the weight attached to the other end of it.

She was even more surprised to find the weight belonged to a bulky black camera case.

Chapter Seventeen

An unconvincing voice in Lily's head suggested it might not be Vinny's camera. Maybe there was a perfectly good reason for someone to store their expensive camera in the garden shed. Admittedly, she struggled to think what that reason might be, but she didn't want to rule out the idea entirely.

After removing the camera from its case, she turned it over in her hands, examining the selection of buttons before idly pressing the power button. The display brightened, showing her own shoes. Taking an educated guess, she pressed the play button, pulling up the last photo taken – that of a sunset over the water from a beach.

With a press of an arrow, she scrolled to the next photo – Alanna leaning against a wall with a bright smile on her face. Then more photos of Alanna. All artfully shot with the stunning scenery from the islands in the background. The pictures were mesmerising enough that, for a few moments, Lily was unconcerned that she was scrolling through the snaps of a man who was now dead.

In her hands was the apparently lost – but now almost certainly stolen – camera of a dead man.

She'd need to hand it in to the police, she thought, retrieving the case to pack the camera away again. She didn't quite get that far. The collection of memory cards slotted into a clear pouch on the inside of the case caught her attention, and curiosity had her pulling them out. Each had a label, and she recognised the names of the other islands in the archipelago – Bryher, Tresco, St Agnes, St Martin's.

Another label contained only a crudely drawn smiley face. The crooked mouth gave it a sinister air, which immediately intrigued Lily. She turned the camera to locate the slot for the memory card.

Once she had it in place, she returned to the display screen. The picture that appeared made Lily's breath catch in her throat.

Her heart raced.

Not only was the photo darker in hue, but it was also darker in nature. Gone was the sense of calm and happiness that the previous pictures evoked.

A chill crept up Lily's spine.

The photo had been taken indoors. It was of a young woman, but not Alanna. This woman looked far younger. Crude lighting bounced off the naked skin of her upper body. Her arms hugged her chest, keeping her breasts covered, yet the action made her look even more exposed. Her lips were stretched into an uncertain smile.

Releasing a breath, Lily scrolled to the next photograph and then the next – they were almost identical until she reached the fourth photo. Here, the woman – barely more than a girl, really – was captured from head to toe. She was entirely naked, with her arms hanging limply at her sides. In this one, there was less uncertainty in her features and more fear.

Fear that left Lily feeling repulsed for looking at the photos.

Quickly, she switched the memory cards back. With

everything back how it had been, she could hand the camera into the police.

Hopefully, it wouldn't matter that she'd put her fingerprints all over the evidence.

The word *evidence* reverberated around her brain as she shifted the camera back into the case. What did this even mean? She'd already thought a stolen camera the day before Vinny's death was an odd coincidence, but now she'd seen what the camera contained, her mind went haywire.

It can't have been an accident. The photographs were motive. A motive for someone to kill him.

With her nerves on tenterhooks, the voice from the garden almost had Lily jumping out of her skin.

"Rodney!" This time she recognised the voice as Oscar's.

In a state of absolute panic, Lily froze.

What should she do? Tell Oscar she'd found the camera. That seemed logical. Except if someone *had* killed Vinny she'd rather not risk the perpetrator knowing she was on to them.

Impulsively, she pushed the camera back into the hidden corner of the shelf. Then she turned and came face to face with Oscar.

"Hi," she said, hoping she didn't seem as nervous as she felt.

"Is everything okay?" Silhouetted in the doorway, he stared at her with eyes full of questions.

"Yes." She blew out a breath and pressed a hand to her breastbone. "The cat almost gave me a heart attack. Did it pass you?"

He shook his head.

"It must have got locked in here," she went on, speaking slightly too fast. "I heard a noise and came to investigate. It knocked the spade over and scarpered." She forced her facial muscles to relax. "That took a few years off my life."

He was only a teenager, and a slight one at that, but his unwavering stare unnerved her.

"It *was* locked in here by mistake?" she asked. "Or have I just lost the cat?"

He shook his head again, as though clearing his thoughts. "She probably slipped in this morning when I was here. She does that sometimes. But she's an outdoor cat. Comes and goes as she pleases."

"Phew." Lily released another breath. "I was worried I'd set her free by mistake."

"No, it's fine." As though remembering his manners, he smiled lightly. "How are you today?"

"I'm good." She moved past him, relieved to be out in the fresh air. "How are you?"

"Okay, I guess."

She cast him a quizzical look.

"Sorry." He frowned and followed her back along the side of the house. "I keep thinking about Vinny. I didn't know him, but I can't stop thinking about him. Did you hear they can't find his family?"

"Really?" Lily sat back down in her seat on the patio, surprised by the openness of the conversation and finding it hard to concentrate with her mind on the camera.

"I assume it will just take time for them to track someone down. He must have family, right? And friends? There must be people who care about him who don't know he's dead."

She swallowed the lump in her throat as she pondered who would be contacted if she died.

Of course she had acquaintances but her unconventional upbringing hadn't been conducive to making lasting friendships. The trend had remained in adulthood.

There were some friends, mostly acquired through her string of unfulfilling jobs, but after her uncle died she'd left her job at the indoor climbing centre and cut off the few friends she'd had. It occurred to her now that it perhaps wasn't a great reflection of the strength of the friendships that she'd been able to cut them off so easily.

Would anyone even notice if she died? Her landlady eventually. Maybe her neighbour, but she was so used to Lily's odd comings and goings that it would probably take her several weeks to think her absence strange.

"Do you want another coffee or anything?" Oscar asked.

She declined with a shake of her head and a grateful smile.

She didn't need more coffee. What she needed was a moment of privacy so she could call the police and report the whereabouts of the missing camera and its chilling contents.

Chapter Eighteen

When Oscar moved away to potter around the far end of the garden, Lily remained on the patio to make her phone call. Annoyingly, all she got was an automated message telling her there was no one to take her call and advising her to call 999 in an emergency. Her other options were to send an email or call back later. The matter wasn't an emergency, but she felt it warranted more urgency than sending an email.

She supposed the dead body had caused a lot of admin work for the small police force. Even if she did get through to them on the phone, they might not be able to come out immediately.

The solution she came up with was to retrieve the camera herself and take it to the police station. That way she could be sure the matter got the attention it deserved.

Her eyes landed on Oscar, cutting back a bush. She'd have to wait for him to leave, so she could go back into the shed unnoticed. Maybe the subterfuge wasn't necessary but she couldn't shake the notion that if there was a killer at large, it was surely better not to alert them to the fact that she was on to them.

The thought that someone at the B&B might have killed

Vinny gave her a chill. She couldn't comprehend that any of them could really commit murder. Perhaps it had been an argument that got out of hand. That seemed more likely than anything premeditated. Except, they'd stolen his camera first, so it clearly wasn't entirely impulsive.

As far as Lily could tell, Oscar was regularly in and out of the shed. Also, she could have sworn she saw a look of panic in his eyes at finding her in there. Equally, he could just have been confused about finding a guest in the shed. He'd also been quite open with her about being shaken up by Vinny's death, so maybe that was what she'd seen in his features, rather than anything to do with the missing camera.

The Millers also had access to the shed. In fact, given that it was only secured with a sliding bolt, anyone could've hidden the camera in there. Maybe whoever did it, had done so entirely impulsively, and the shed was merely a convenient place to stash it in the short term.

Then again, the photos suggested whoever had stolen it hadn't done it purely on impulse, but with a motive. Surely it would be a strange coincidence if the theft had nothing to do with the lewd pictures.

It occurred to her that if she'd known what was on the camera maybe she'd have stolen it too. Perhaps whoever took it had intended to pass it on to the police to investigate its contents.

Which begged the question of why they hadn't done that. Had they been deterred by his death? Or had they broached the matter with him and the conversation had ended up with him dead?

That was, of course, if whoever took it was as repulsed by the photographs as she was. It was hard to imagine anyone not being, but it was also hard to imagine what kind of person took those kinds of photos in the first place.

One like Vinny, apparently.

"Are you sure you don't want another coffee?" Oscar asked, appearing before her and breaking her thoughts.

"No, thanks."

"I'm more than happy to grab you one before I head out... or something else to drink?"

She smiled politely as she declined again. "Are you leaving?"

"Yes. I'm done for the day. At least at this job. I have a shift at the Star Castle Hotel in an hour."

Lily's eyebrows rose. "You're busy."

"Keeps me out of mischief," he said with a cheeky smile. "Anyway, I'll probably see you tomorrow."

She said goodbye and watched him disappear around the side of the house. Intently, she listened to him returning his gardening tools to the shed. As soon as it went quiet, she'd fetch the camera.

With a rush of adrenaline, she took tentative steps to the side of the house and caught sight of the back of Oscar before he disappeared along the lane.

Now was her chance. She'd grab the stolen goods and hand them in to PC Grainger with no one noticing.

"Hello, dear!" a friendly voice greeted her.

Turning, she tried to keep the disappointment from her face. "Hi, Mrs Miller."

"Please..." She waved a hand in front of her face. "It's Flora. I see you're enjoying the garden."

"Yes." She took steps back towards the table and chairs.

"It'll do you the world of good being out in the fresh air, even if it is such a miserable day. Best not to keep yourself hidden away in your room. Not after yesterday. We all need to keep our spirits up." She smiled sadly. "That sounds harsh, doesn't it? But life is for the living, isn't that what they say? And seeing death so close puts life into perspective. We need to make the most of every moment. Don't let what happened yesterday stop you from enjoying your holiday."

"I'll try not to," she said, deciding not to mention that she wasn't really on holiday.

A holiday implied some sort of break from everyday life. She didn't have a normal life to take a break from. It occurred to her briefly that inheriting enough money that she might never need to work again may not be quite the luxury it sounded. Having to work would probably be a good thing. It would give her life some structure at least.

Broken from her thoughts, Lily frowned at the sound of Alanna's high-pitched voice as she joined them on the patio.

"This weather is unbelievable," she said, glaring at Mrs Miller as though it was entirely her fault. "I feel like a prisoner. We even tried to book a helicopter to get off the island, but they refuse to fly, same as the planes. It's ridiculous. I've suffered a trauma and I want to go home."

"It's dangerous to fly in this weather," Mrs Miller said. "But fog like this never stays long. Especially not in the spring. It'll be a few days at the most."

"*A few days!*" Alanna shrieked, then switched her gaze to Marc, who was leaning in the doorway. "She says it might take a few days. What are we going to do for a few days?"

He shrugged. "Just wait, I guess. What else can we do?"

Lily could empathise about waiting. How long would she have to wait for everyone to clear out so she could get back into the shed? Since it didn't seem it was going to happen anytime soon, she slipped away from the continuing conversation about the weather and went up to the relative peace of her room.

Half an hour later, she heard heavy footsteps on the stairs and shifted to the door to better hear the conversation between Alanna and Marc.

"I can't do anything about the weather," Marc was saying patiently. "And since your attempt at bribing the helicopter pilot didn't work, I'm not sure what else we can do."

"My nerves can't take this." Alanna's voice was only just

audible through the door. "I swear I'm going to have a breakdown."

"We'll be home before you know it," Marc said. "Why don't you get on with writing that post about Vinny for your followers..."

Lily caught Alanna saying something about her fans missing her before the voices trailed off. Moving to the window, she spotted Mr and Mrs Miller in the garden – heads bent together as they chatted by the wall. That thwarted her plans to go back to the shed.

To kill some time, she set out in search of food. She spent an hour in a cafe at the other side of the island, and the daylight was fading when she returned to the house.

Bypassing the front door, she slipped stealthily around the side of the house and made straight for the shed. Quietly, she slid the bolt and opened the door. She'd be in and out within moments, then walk straight back to Hugh Town and the police station.

Except when she moved the plant pots aside, there was no sign of the camera.

Against logic, she pushed her hand into the corner and fumbled around as though she might have just missed it.

Nothing.

Frantically, she moved around the shed, checking every inch of shelf space.

Still nothing.

The camera was gone.

Chapter Nineteen

TUESDAY

After spending most of the night tossing and turning, Lily finally fell into a deep sleep just as the sun was rising, then woke with a start hours later.

Frantically, she hopped out of bed and pulled on jeans and a hoodie. She'd tried calling the police again the previous evening but had once again had no luck.

Now, she cursed herself for not trying harder to get in touch with them. She could have called the emergency number and asked them to pass on a message, or tried messaging through their social media site, as the locals apparently did.

There was no sense worrying about that now. She'd try an in-person visit to the station and hope the place was manned.

A rush of relief hit her when she swept the bedroom curtains aside. The fog remained, meaning Alanna and Marc wouldn't have been able to leave the island yet. It felt suddenly imperative that no one went anywhere until the police had got to the bottom of all of this.

The power walk along the quiet lanes got Lily's blood pumping and she felt a rush of anticipation when she approached the police station.

Distracted, she didn't immediately see the Millers lingering outside the building. It was the voices that drew her attention.

"I'd like to get on the next ferry," Flora said to her husband. "After all this, I need a break. As soon as the weather clears, we'll go over and spend a week or two with Kerry and Jim."

"We can't both go," Rodney argued. "We have guests."

"I'm going to cancel the bookings." Sniffing, Flora dabbed a tissue under her eyes.

"You can't just cancel bookings. Especially not at such short notice. Are you trying to ruin us?"

Flora opened her mouth to reply, but spotted Lily and smiled gently instead. "Hello, love," she said. "Such a shame about the weather. Hopefully it'll clear soon so you can properly explore the islands."

"Yes," Lily said, glancing past them at the door of the police station.

"Were you coming to see PC Grainger?" Rodney asked.

"Umm..." She hesitated. "Yes. I wanted to check in and see if he had any more questions for me or anything."

"You can't stop thinking about all this business either, I take it?" Rodney said. "Poor Oscar is the same. We had to give him the day off because he's so shaken by the whole thing."

"Terrible," Flora muttered. "Life goes on, though. Make every moment count. It just makes me want to be with my daughter and grandchildren."

Rodney's eye roll was subtle, but Lily caught it all the same. "PC Grainger is there now," he said, standing aside to let Lily pass.

"See you later," she said, managing a weak smile as she left them.

"Hi," PC Grainger said, looking up from his computer screen.

"Morning," she said, then glanced at her watch, happy to find it *was* still morning.

He flicked a hand toward the chair opposite him. "How can I help you?"

"I wanted to talk to you about the camera. Vinny's camera," she clarified. "The stolen one."

He nodded slowly. "I haven't contacted his sister yet, but when we do, his belongings will be returned to her. The camera included."

Lily blinked rapidly. "What?"

"His sister is his next of kin, so his things will go to her."

"Including the camera?" she asked, confused.

"Yes."

"But..." Her mind whirred. "The camera is lost."

"It turned up." The tilt of his head made it clear that he'd assumed she knew that.

"It can't have turned up," she said. "What do you mean?"

"Mr and Mrs Miller have just handed it in. Apparently, it was misplaced all along."

Lily struggled to get her brain to catch up. "Where was it found?" Presumably the Millers had also stumbled across it in the shed. Whoever had stashed it there must be kicking themselves for their poor hiding spot.

"In the neighbour's garden," PC Grainger said. "At the time it got lost I understand furniture was being moved around. I guess Vinny set it down on the garden wall and it got knocked off."

"No," Lily said on a quick inhale.

"Excuse me?" PC Grainger said.

"It was in the shed. Someone hid it in the shed. Have you checked the photos on it?"

"I had a quick look," he said, eyes drifting to the bulky camera case on the sideboard, which Lily hadn't noticed until now. "It's all work photos."

"The other memory cards," Lily said in a rush. "Did you look at them?"

"No," he said slowly. "I just had a brief glance over the labels. It appears it was all from his work trip on the islands."

"There's one with a smiley face on the label," Lily told him. "You need to look at that one."

"I didn't notice anything like that." He slid his chair back and reached for the camera bag.

"Aren't you supposed to wear gloves?" she asked as he lifted the camera out and set it on the desk.

His eyes narrowed, but he didn't look up from the camera case. "This isn't CSI."

"Clearly," she muttered.

One corner of his lips twitched into a smirk. He lay out the memory cards between them. "I don't see anything unusual," he remarked.

"I don't understand." Lily sifted through them. "It's not here."

"What isn't?"

"There was another memory card and it had different photos on it..."

"Different how?"

"Photos of a naked woman," she said. "Girl really. A teenager, I guess. She looked young and..." She winced. "It didn't seem as though she wanted to be photographed."

PC Grainger sat up straighter. "And you saw these photographs *when,* exactly?"

"Yesterday. I found the camera in the shed at the Miller's place."

He frowned. "The Millers found it this morning at the other side of the garden wall."

"That's not where it was yesterday."

"Why didn't you report this yesterday?"

"Because I panicked and hid it again. I tried to call you but there was no answer so I decided to wait until there was no one around and get the camera to bring it to you. But when I went back for it in the evening, it wasn't there any more."

"Weird," PC Grainger said, twisting his lips to one side. "You looked through the photos yesterday?"

"Yes." She glanced down at the selection of memory cards again. "There was another one."

"Having naked pictures isn't a crime," he pointed out. "Maybe it was a girlfriend."

"I really don't think so. The woman was really young and she looked scared. Also, if it was perfectly innocent, why would someone hide it?"

"And why would the camera have been in the shed and then magically appear behind the garden wall?" he mused.

"Exactly," Lily said, feeling validated by the flicker of excitement in PC Grainger's eyes.

"This all sounds quite suspicious," he said.

"Do you think the photographs had something to do with his death?" The edge of excitement in Lily's voice was probably quite inappropriate.

"I don't know." His rubbed at his jaw. "This clearly needs further investigation. I need to make some calls, then I'll get back to you. In the meantime, I don't think you should speak to anyone about what you've just told me. No doubt I'll need to interview you again later, but for now just don't go far. Okay?"

"Thanks to the fog, that isn't even possible." She hopped out of her seat. "I'll be at the bed and breakfast, but you also have my number. I'll talk to you later."

Chapter Twenty

Flynn had intended to update Sergeant Proctor on the camera situation via a message, but given what Miss Larkin had told him, he decided a phone call was warranted.

The phone rang for quite some time before Sergeant Proctor's rough voice greeted him.

"How are you feeling?" Flynn asked politely.

"Probably about as good as I sound. Has something happened?"

"There's been a development I thought you ought to know about. Regarding the stolen camera. It was handed in this morning by Mr and Mrs Miller. It'd been found by the young lad who does the gardening for them."

"Good. That sounds like a loose end tied up. You could have sent me a message."

"Except I'm not sure it ties anything up," PC Grainger told him. "I've just had a chat with Miss Larkin. She told me she discovered the camera hidden in the garden shed yesterday and that there were images of a naked woman on one of the memory cards."

A heavy sigh came down the phone. "Nude photos aren't necessarily a crime."

"I realise that, but from the way Miss Larkin described them, I suspect these were the criminal variety."

"And what did *you* think?"

"How do you mean?"

"What's your opinion of the photographs?"

"I haven't seen them."

"Why not?"

"They've disappeared. When Lily went back to retrieve the camera from the shed yesterday evening, it had been moved. This morning, the Millers handed it in claiming that Oscar found it in the neighbour's garden."

"That sounds messy."

"Yeah. Something doesn't add up. And if Mr Roth has been up to something shady, that adds a whole new spin to his death."

"That seems like a leap." Sergeant Proctor cleared his throat. "We have Mr Roth's possessions, don't we?"

"Yes. Alanna and her boyfriend packed up his things. They brought them in yesterday. I still haven't managed to contact the next of kin, by the way."

"Have a squiz through his belongings and see if anything jumps out at you."

PC Grainger was already on his feet and moving to the storeroom at the back of the building. "Will do. I'll let you know if I find anything."

He located Mr Roth's belongings easily. A large duffel bag and a backpack. After donning a pair of gloves he had a quick rummage through the duffel, but it was only clothes and shoes. Nothing out of place there. But then, surely anything valuable would be stashed in his backpack.

Everything seemed to be in order with his wallet, and nothing jumped out as suspicious. He'd thought perhaps there'd be more memory cards, but so far there was nothing. After continuing to probe the smaller pockets, he came across a mobile phone, but that was no help without the passcode.

Presumably his laptop would be password protected too, but if not, that could be quite revealing. Not that he should really be delving into the devices. The digital forensic team should be the ones to deal with it, but given that the death was currently being classed as an accident, he wasn't too concerned about breaking protocol.

Abruptly, Flynn stopped his search of the backpack. Then he looked again before concluding that there really was no laptop lurking inside.

There was no way he'd have been travelling without a laptop. Surely he needed one for the job. After re-packing the bag, Flynn wandered back to his desk and found the number for Alanna Harding. He didn't have to wait long for her to answer the phone, and exchanged a polite greeting with her before getting to the point.

"I wonder if you know if Mr Roth had a laptop with him?" he asked.

"Yes," she said without hesitation. "Of course. Why?"

"Because there isn't one among his belongings, so I'm just wondering what happened to it. Do you have it?"

"No. I didn't think about it when we packed his things. My head was all over the place, but now that you mention it, I didn't see it. Hang on a sec and I'll ask Marc if he knows anything about it."

PC Grainger waited while she filled her boyfriend in. A moment later, she put the phone on speaker.

"I didn't see it," Marc told him. "But we also didn't look too hard. Now I'm wondering if he might have hidden it somewhere."

"Why would he hide his laptop?" Alanna asked.

"His camera had been stolen," Marc said. "Or that's what he thought. Maybe he was worried about security."

"That makes sense," PC Grainger said.

"Do you want us to have another look around his room?" Alanna asked.

"Yes, please." He could go and search himself, but he'd really like to know the whereabouts of it as soon as possible.

They stayed on the phone and PC Grainger listened while they searched under the mattress and behind the bed, and in all the other nooks and crannies.

"That's really weird," Alanna said. "Where on earth could it be?"

"Maybe he had it with him when he went out that morning," Marc suggested.

"We carried out a sweep of the surrounding area," PC Grainger mused. "Nothing was found." A laptop shouldn't be too difficult to spot, either. "Thanks for checking his room," he said. "If it turns up, please let me know."

They promised they would, and he ended the call even more confused than he had been before.

Over a coffee, he sat and pondered what he knew, but couldn't make sense of it.

He gave himself until the bottom of the coffee before he called the sergeant again.

"Anything turn up?" Sergeant Proctor asked gruffly.

"Not exactly. I couldn't find anything incriminating in his belongings, but I noticed a lack of a laptop. I thought it strange that he wouldn't have one, so I called Alanna. She confirmed he had one, and she checked his room again. It's not there. She doesn't know where it could be."

"Right. So what you're saying is, you have no evidence of anything? That's actually a good outcome for your search."

"How so?"

"Because with no evidence, we don't need to do anything."

"But his laptop is missing," Flynn pointed out. "That's a sign of something dodgy."

"All you keep telling me is what you don't have. I'm not sure what kind of policing you're used to, but around here we build a case based on evidence, not a lack thereof."

"Come on," Flynn said, more fiercely than he'd intended.

"You have to admit that something isn't adding up here." He had a nasty suspicion that Sergeant Proctor might dismiss anything Flynn said out of spite, regardless of whether he thought he was right or wrong.

"There is nothing to suggest that what happened to Mr Roth was anything other than an accident," Sergeant Proctor said slowly, as though talking to a child. "So that is exactly how we're going to treat it."

Flynn stood and paced the room. "Can we please keep this professional? Put aside your feelings about me and look at this objectively."

"That's exactly what I am doing," the sergeant snapped, then spluttered and coughed. "And I'll tell you something about policing around here. It's nothing like what you're used to. It's a quiet, peaceful place with good people—"

"That doesn't mean you should turn a blind eye to a potential crime."

"Stop and think for a minute, will you?" Sergeant Proctor growled. "What you're suggesting is that Mr Roth's death wasn't an accident. You know what that leads to... a murder investigation. And what do you think a murder investigation does to a place like this? A place where most businesses survive on visitors to the island. Imagine what happens when all those holidaymakers decide not to visit because there's talk of a murder. Even if it turns out not to be true, the bad publicity will stick."

"You can't be serious," Flynn whispered, dropping into his seat.

"Don't push this," the sergeant said, a warning note in his voice. "If you think you're on my bad side now, I should warn you that things could get way worse for you." He paused. "Are we clear?"

"Crystal," Flynn said flatly, then hung up the phone, only barely resisting the urge to fling it across the room.

Chapter Twenty-One

In anticipation of spending some time holed up in her room, Lily bought a bunch of snacks from the supermarket before making her way back to the bed and breakfast.

After a couple of hours, she got bored with looking at the same four walls. Since the house was quiet, she ventured downstairs and made herself a cup of tea in the breakfast room. Taking it to the living room, she took a seat, then pulled out a heavy book on Cornwall's wildlife from the shelf under the coffee table. The photos were stunning, making Lily think of Vinny and his talent for photography. A pang of sadness hit her until an image of the naked girl came back to her, leaving a jolt of anger in its place.

Even if it turned out he was a criminal, he didn't deserve to die, she told herself. And if his death wasn't an accident, the truth should be known. She checked her watch, wishing PC Grainger would at least keep her updated with what was happening.

The sound of the doorbell had her setting the book aside and craning her neck to listen as Mrs Miller's footsteps sounded through the breakfast room and along the hall. The voices were muffled, prompting Lily to move closer to the doorway.

"I think she's here," Mrs Miller was saying. "Upstairs, as far as I know. I can check..."

Lily poked her head around the doorframe.

"There she is," PC Grainger said, removing his hat as he stepped inside. He locked eyes with Lily. "I just need a quick word with you about your witness statement. Is now a good time?"

"Yes. Of course."

"It shouldn't take long. Can we use the living room?" he asked Flora.

"Of course. Can I get you a cuppa or anything?"

He declined and moved purposefully into the living room with Lily, closing the door behind him.

"It's not an issue that my fingerprints are on the camera, is it?" Lily asked, lowering herself onto the couch again while PC Grainger sat on the armchair.

"What?"

"I was thinking that if you check the camera for finger-prints you should be able to find out who stole it... but mine will also be on there. And yours and the Miller's. I guess Alanna and Marc could have plausibly handled it, too."

PC Grainger scratched at his forehead and the strain in his eyes gave the impression he might have a headache.

"No one will be checking for fingerprints," he said with a soft sigh.

"Sorry. Have I gone all CSI again? How will the investigation go?"

"There won't be an investigation." He pulled his shoulders back as he sat straighter.

"How come?"

"As things stand there isn't any evidence that the camera was stolen. Just misplaced."

"But it was in the shed," Lily reminded him. "And then magically appeared in the neighbour's garden."

PC Grainger's cheek twitched and he tilted his head.

"And what about the photos I saw?" Lily asked.

"The problem is we don't have those photographs."

"But you have to investigate," Lily said urgently. "Surely you need to examine the possibility that his death wasn't an accident."

"There isn't anything to suggest it was anything other than an accident."

It took her a moment to wrap her head around the unexpected turn of the conversation. "But there is!" Her voice rose. "The photos and the fact that the camera was hidden."

"I'm afraid we can't start an investigation based on hearsay."

"I don't understand." She shook her head and tried to catch his eye, but he seemed determined not to make eye contact. "Are you saying you don't believe me?"

He took a steady breath and appeared to be choosing his words carefully. "I'm sure you can imagine how upsetting it would be for Mr Roth's family if we started an investigation with no evidence to back it up."

Her eyes widened as she realised they really wouldn't look into things further. "I imagine they'd be more upset if they thought there was a chance someone had killed him and you didn't bother to look into it."

"It's been a stressful few days and this is a lot for you to process, but it's a huge leap to suggest someone killed him."

"His camera was stolen," she said slowly. "With some pretty disturbing pictures. And then the guy mysteriously died."

"The wet rocks can be treacherous," he said flatly.

"So people often just fall and die around here when they're out for a walk?" she snapped.

Finally, his gaze met hers. "Unfortunately, accidents happen."

While her blood pulsed hard in her veins, Lily completely lost her cool. "This doesn't make sense. When I spoke to you this morning, you believed me. You agreed that there should be an investigation. What happened between then and now?"

"What happened was I thought about what you'd said and discussed the situation with a colleague. After further consideration, I concluded that there's nothing to investigate."

He stood before he'd even finished speaking and the motion almost had the effect of hiding his irritation. But not quite.

Lily just couldn't figure out where his annoyance was directed.

"You really don't think there's anything suspicious about this whole situation?" she asked while he moved towards the door.

"I think—" As he pushed the back of his hand across his forehead, he looked suddenly exhausted. "I think it would be best if you focussed on enjoying the rest of your holiday."

He didn't look at her again and was gone before she could say anything more.

So she didn't have time to explain that she wasn't on holiday. That she was searching for answers about her childhood. Not that she was too concerned about finding the owner of the ice cream shop now.

She had a new mission.

If the police wouldn't investigate Vinny's death, she'd just have to do their job for them.

Chapter Twenty-Two

ASKING a few questions wouldn't do any harm. It might come to nothing, but Lily knew it would forever bother her if she didn't at least try to find answers.

When Flora wandered into the living room to check on Lily, moments after PC Grainger left, it seemed like a good idea to start with her.

"PC Grainger mentioned the camera had turned up," Lily said, remaining on the couch. "You found it in the neighbour's garden, did you?"

"Not us, no. Oscar found it this morning when he arrived."

Lily frowned. "I thought you'd given him the day off."

"We did. After he found the camera. It shook him up. This whole thing has. So I told him to go home and we went and handed in the camera. I explained that to PC Grainger."

"He only mentioned that you'd handed it in." She chewed on her bottom lip. Oscar finding it actually made more sense, since she'd already suspected he'd been the one to steal it and stash it in the shed. Presumably now he was trying to cover his tracks.

"I'm glad it turned up." Flora sank into the armchair and lowered her voice. "It gave me goosebumps to think of someone stealing from right under our noses. Rodney feels better now that it's turned up, too. He's been quite stressed out recently."

Lily smiled and aimed for a nonchalant tone. "It must be quite demanding to run a bed and breakfast."

"You wouldn't believe," Flora said forcefully. "If you'd have told me two years ago how much stress it would be, I'd never have believed it either."

"I suppose it's rewarding too," Lily ventured.

Flora's reaction was anything but enthusiastic. "You'd think so, wouldn't you? It sounds so idyllic, running a B&B. Mostly it's just hard work with little reward." Her eyes misted over, and Lily stayed quiet, waiting to see if she'd share more. "Sorry," she said with a gentle shake of the head. "This tragedy has made me want to be close to my daughter and grandkids more than ever. They live in Devon so I don't see them as much as I'd like."

"Do you ever think of moving closer to them?" Lily asked, despite already knowing the answer.

"All the time. That's my dream. If only I could convince Rodney. He's been in his element since we opened this place. It's given him a new lease of life. Now I feel as though no matter what we do, only one of us will end up happy."

"I'm sorry," Lily murmured.

"Don't listen to me being all morose." Flora tried for a smile but it wasn't convincing. "I hope the weather improves soon so you can see the island at its best. It's remarkable how different it looks with some blue sky and sunshine."

With a gentle smile, Lily stood up. "Fingers crossed it improves soon." She declined Flora's offer to make her a drink and set off to the privacy of her room to ponder her next move.

Instinct had her knocking on Alanna and Marc's door, but there was no answer. That probably wasn't a bad thing since Lily had no idea what she would say to them.

It was only that the logical thing seemed to be to talk to

everyone who'd interacted with Vinny before his death and see what she came up with.

Someone knew something. She had no doubt about that.

Oscar was the person she most wanted to speak to. If only he hadn't been given the day off.

Like a light bulb illuminating in her brain, Lily remembered him mentioning that he had another job too. At the Star Castle Hotel. Which surely couldn't be too hard for her to locate. On a surge of adrenaline, she grabbed her jacket and headed back out of her room.

With her mind elsewhere, she didn't notice the person at the bottom of the stairs until she almost collided with her. The teenage girl didn't pay Lily any attention in her hurry to get out of the front door. Even at the speed she was moving Lily caught the tears which streamed from her bloodshot eyes.

She opened her mouth to ask if she was okay, but the girl was gone before she could formulate words.

Along the hall, Alanna stood in the doorway to the living room.

"Is she okay?" Lily asked, pointing behind her.

Alanna shrugged. "She was looking for her boyfriend."

"Boyfriend?" Lily parroted.

"That kid who works here."

"Oscar?"

"I guess so." Alanna shrugged again.

It dawned on Lily that the girl was the same one who'd been chatting to Oscar a few days earlier. She'd seemed agitated then, too.

"Why was she so upset?" she asked, as Alanna passed her and started up the stairs.

"Who knows?" she replied without looking back.

Chapter Twenty-Three

WALKING AT A BRISK PACE, Lily reached Hugh Town quickly. As she passed Mr Greaves' office, her mind briefly flicked to the other mystery – of why the owner of the ice cream shop was intent on shrouding herself in secrecy. She'd come back to that conundrum later. First, she had a destination in mind for a late lunch.

The Star Castle Hotel sat high on the hill, overlooking the harbour, and reached by a steep, narrow lane. With a choice of restaurants, Lily opted for the one in the conservatory and admired the twisted grape vines which hung overhead. On a sunny day it must have been stunning, but the lingering fog gave a cold feel despite the temperature being comfortable.

There was no sign of Oscar, but Lily kept an eye out while she tucked into her salmon salad. She declined coffee and dessert, choosing instead to pay her bill and explore the rest of the hotel.

The bar seemed a good place to sit and observe. A few people were seated nearby, and more came and went through the reception area.

Lily was almost at the bottom of her sparkling water when she finally spotted Oscar crossing the foyer. With his phone in his hand, he was too distracted to notice Lily, and she kept her gaze on him as he hovered by the reception desk.

After tapping away on his phone, he raised it to his ear then paced a few steps back and forth before shoving it roughly into his pocket. With hunched shoulders he left quickly through the main entrance. Lily offered the waiter a quick smile of farewell as she snatched her bag from beside her feet and made a dash for it.

Oscar hadn't gone far. He leaned against the stone wall, staring at the boats bobbing in the harbour below.

"Hey!" Lily called cheerfully as she approached.

His fingers drummed against his thigh when he turned, and it took a moment for recognition to hit his eyes. "Oh, hi."

"I had lunch in the restaurant," she told him.

"Nice," he muttered and turned away again.

Lily moved to stand beside him. "I heard you found Vinny's camera."

"Yeah." He paused before saying more. "Do you think that sometimes things work out as they're supposed to?" His voice had a faraway quality, as though he was thinking out loud.

"Maybe," she whispered, but he didn't seem to be waiting for a reply.

"Like sometimes when people die, it's for the best..."

Unsure how to respond, Lily merely gave a quiet hum of acknowledgement.

He shook his head and looked at her. "I'm not saying he deserved to die or anything... but..." He cleared his throat. "Some people... well, some people aren't very nice. Maybe Vinny wasn't very nice?" It came out as a question and he was suddenly staring at Lily as though she might have all the answers.

"Maybe." She smiled sadly. "I only encountered him a couple of times, but I didn't find him at all pleasant."

"I think he hated women," Oscar said, looking towards the horizon again. "And I think he was a bully."

Lily nodded. "I saw your girlfriend earlier," she told him.

"I don't have a girlfriend," he said, surprise wrinkling his forehead.

"The girl I saw you with the other day..."

"Katie?" His eyes bored into Lily's. "Where was she?"

"At the B&B. She looked upset."

He swore under his breath. "When was this? Where is she now?"

"I don't know. She was leaving when I saw her."

"And she was upset?"

"She was crying. I think she'd been talking to Alanna."

He swore again and pressed a button on his phone before holding it to his ear. "She won't answer my calls," he muttered.

Lily had a whole bunch of questions, but what she really wanted to know was if he'd been the one to steal the camera and if he knew about the missing memory card. Before she could ask a question, a tall woman stalked out of the hotel entrance and called out to Oscar.

"The room service won't deliver itself," she bellowed. "Are you working today or not? Because I'd appreciate it if you could get your head out of the clouds."

Oscar moved the phone from his ear but continued to stare at it in his hand. "No. I can't work today." His gaze flicked up to the woman. "I'm sorry. I'm not feeling well. I have to go."

The woman shouted after him, but he didn't look back as he rushed away down the steep street.

Lily followed him, but he broke into a run. By the time she reached the lane at the bottom of the slope, she'd lost sight of him entirely.

Chapter Twenty-Four

THE WALK from the hotel to the Mermaid Inn only took a few minutes. Lily pushed the door open and her eyes did a quick sweep of the nautical themed decorations before landing on the exact person she'd been looking for.

"I was hoping to find you here," Lily said, sliding onto the stool beside Seren.

"It's kind of sad how easy I am to track down." She smiled widely and gave Lily an affectionate pat on the shoulder in greeting. "I'm not even working and I'm still here. But in my defence, I just finished a shift. I was waiting to see if Kit might appear, but I guess he's already at home." Her features turned serious. "How are you doing? Are you managing to enjoy your holiday?"

That word again. She was staying in a B&B for a week in a popular holiday destination so she supposed it made sense that people assumed she was on holiday. Maybe she should take it as a sign that she should use the rest of her time on the island to relax. She didn't seem to be very good at that, though. It suited her much better to have something to do rather than sitting around doing nothing.

"It's fine," she said. "Probably not most people's idea of a holiday, but it's really okay."

"Glad to hear it. Were you looking for me for something specific, or did you just want to hang out? Shall I get us a glass of wine?" She was off her seat and behind the bar in an instant.

Deciding she needed to keep a clear head, Lily passed on the wine and opted for water instead.

"I wanted to ask you a question," she said, then waited for Seren to pour her drink and return to sit beside her.

"Go on then," Seren said. "What's the question?"

When she opened her mouth, Lily felt torn. "To be honest, I have two questions... the first is about the ice cream shop. I was wondering if you can think of anyone who might know the owner. I tried asking the solicitor like Kit suggested, but he couldn't tell me much. He wouldn't even give me a name. He was weirdly secretive, but I feel as though someone around here must at least know the name of the owner."

Seren looked thoughtful, then swivelled on her stool to look at the guy serving customers on the other side of the room. "Noah?" she called as he walked towards the bar. "Do you remember the name of the woman who owned the old ice cream shop on the promenade?"

"Nope," he replied, dashing Lily's hopes. "Mum would probably know, though. Why?"

"Lily's interested," Seren said, tipping her head.

Noah held out his hand and introduced himself. "You're the one who found the dead body?" he asked quietly.

"That's me," she said with a wry smile.

"Noah is Kit's brother," Seren explained. "And he's right that Mirren might remember the owner of the ice cream shop. I'll message her and ask." She tapped rapidly on her phone. "What was the other question?"

"Do you happen to know the young guy who works at the B&B? Oscar."

Seren nodded. "Oscar Morris. I know *of* him. His dad is in here often."

"Do you know how I might go about finding Oscar?" Hopefully, Seren wouldn't find the question too strange.

"I know where he lives," she said. "That's as much as I could tell you."

"That would be helpful." Lily caught the questioning dip of Seren's eyebrows. "I saw him earlier, and he was upset about the guy who died, but he rushed away before I could talk to him properly. Also, I saw his girlfriend earlier and she was in tears. I just want to check they're okay."

"See!" Noah quipped, eyes on Seren. "*Some people* are upset about his death."

"I didn't say no one was upset," Seren huffed, shaking her head. "Just that not *everyone* is."

"What?" Lily asked, narrowing her eyes.

Seren shifted to face her. "Last night I saw Alanna had posted about the guy's death on her social media accounts, and as I was scrolling through the comments. One woman posted this nasty message, basically saying she was glad he was dead."

"Really?" Automatically, Lily got her phone out and opened social media to look for Alanna's account.

"It's not there any more," Seren said. "Alanna must have removed it. But it makes you wonder what kind of person he was, if there are people out there who are happy he's dead."

Noah shook his head and leaned his elbows on the bar. "I told you, it's internet trolls. Some people enjoy leaving nasty comments. It says nothing about the guy. I'll bet if I were to die and you posted about it, there'd be someone crop up saying good riddance too."

"True." Seren's lips twitched into a mischievous grin. "That'd be me!"

Reaching across the bar, Noah shoved a hand into her hair and ruffled it with all the affection of an annoying sibling. In response, Seren shoved his hand away with similar affection.

"It's not actually true though," Seren said. "You have to really have enemies for someone to say something bad about you after you're dead."

"The person probably didn't even know him," Noah insisted.

Lily's head was bent over her phone. She'd located Alanna's post about Vinny, all heartfelt and gushy. The comments beneath it were full of sympathy.

"She worded it a bit weirdly," Lily mused. "The post is all about her... It's like she's using his death for her own benefit."

"I thought that too." Seren took a swig of her Coke. "There's something quite insincere about the tone of it, but if you look through her other posts, nothing sounds very genuine. I'm not sure how she has such a massive following."

"Probably because she's fit," Noah said, straightening up.

Seren rolled her eyes. "Can I tell your girlfriend you said that?"

"Probably better if you don't." He seemed to mull it over before he gave a subtle shrug. "Although Keira's pretty cute when she's jealous."

"I don't think Alanna's that attractive," Lily said, lifting her eyes from her phone. "Plus, I guess most of her followers are women."

"The women want to be her," Noah said. "The men want to..." His lips twitched mischievously. "Be *with* her," he ventured.

Lily really couldn't see his point of view. "I don't understand why people are drawn to someone so insincere."

"It's all about image," Noah said. "A lot of people are sucked in by all these perfect photos. They want to believe that Alanna has a perfect life. If she has a perfect life, it gives them something to aspire to."

"Maybe," Lily conceded. "But there's something fishy if you ask me."

"How do you mean?" Seren asked.

Realising what she'd said, Lily shook her head. "Nothing. Never mind."

Seren dipped her head and lowered her voice. "Something fishy about Alanna's social media post?"

"No." Lily winced. "Ignore me. I shouldn't say anything."

"Well, now you have to tell us," Noah said, leaning in.

She hesitated and instinctively glanced around before speaking. "I had this feeling that maybe Vinny's death wasn't an accident. I mentioned it to PC Grainger this morning, and it seemed as though he was going to look into it... but this afternoon he did a complete turnaround and said there was nothing to investigate."

The pair of them stared at her as though they weren't comprehending her.

Noah frowned deeply. "But if it wasn't an accident..." He trailed off and shook his head.

"You think someone killed him?" Seren whispered.

"It sounds ridiculous, I know." She smiled, hoping they wouldn't think she was mad. "I'm probably way off the mark, but something just feels off about the whole thing."

Seren eyed her sympathetically. "It must have been really horrible to be the one to find him."

"Was there something about the way you found him that made you think it wasn't an accident?" Noah asked, seeming more willing to believe her than Seren.

"No, it's not that." She forced a smile. "You're probably right – it was just the shock of finding him that has sent my mind racing."

"I didn't mean to be dismissive," Seren said. "If you really think there's more to it, speak to PC Grainger again. Make him listen to you."

"I'm sure he'd look into it further if you convinced him there was a reason to," Noah agreed.

Seren tucked her chin. "Is that why you wanted to speak to Oscar?"

"Kind of. He seems like a sweet kid and I was worried about him when I saw him earlier." He'd definitely seemed cagey, just as he'd done when he'd found Lily in the shed. There was also the time she'd seen him with his friend outside the B&B when Vinny's camera had gone missing—

Lily's eyes felt as though they might fall out of her head as that encounter came back to her. The two of them had been talking secretively. Something about someone being a creep and Oscar talking about going to the police about it.

Of course! It was them who'd taken the camera, and they clearly knew about the seedy photos. But what on earth had they done with the memory card?

She needed to speak to Oscar and find out.

Schooling her features to disguise her panic, she looked at Seren. "If you don't mind giving me Oscar's address, I think I'll call over and see if he's okay."

"Of course." Seren looked at her phone screen. "I didn't hear back from Mirren yet. Do you want to give me your number and I'll let you know when she replies?"

They exchanged numbers and Seren showed her Oscar's place on the map. His parent's place. An old farmhouse on the eastern side of the island.

Lily thanked Seren for her help and left the comfort of the welcoming pub.

Out on the street, she stopped short as her eyes landed on PC Grainger across the road. He didn't notice her, his gaze not leaving the blonde woman who whispered in his ear. The same woman he'd been in the pub with the other evening.

She had her hand on his arm and her breasts pushed inappropriately close to his chest. Not that Lily would usually judge the closeness between a couple, but he was in uniform. It didn't make for the most professional vibe.

Even if they were a *proper* couple it wouldn't be appropriate, but as far as Lily could make out, the woman was just one in a string of flings.

It wasn't right that he was neglecting his duties to the public in favour of looking down some woman's top.

Irritated, Lily didn't bother to avert her gaze when PC Grainger finally looked up, and instead glared at him with overt disgust.

He didn't even have the decency to look contrite. Just stared back at her with a glint of humour in his eyes. He maintained eye contact for too long, only breaking it when he had a hand on the small of his friend's back to encourage her along in the opposite direction.

Lily seethed.

Chapter Twenty-Five

EVEN IF HE weren't on duty, the way Michaela draped herself over Flynn would have made him uncomfortable. Public displays of affection weren't really his thing. Especially not with some woman he'd spent one night with and wasn't even a hundred percent sure of her name. He had Michaela in his head, but maybe it was Melissa. He was sure it began with M and ended in A. Marianna, perhaps.

Since he hadn't expected to see her again, learning her name hadn't felt necessary. They hadn't swapped numbers, and since she was only visiting the islands for a holiday, he'd been confident that their one-night stand would be just that.

But she'd approached him on the street, acting as though they were old friends and whispering in his ear about how much she'd enjoyed their night together. He could have taken a step back, reminded her he was on duty and fed her some lie about catching up with her later. But that would require him to care about appearances.

If he cared about that, he wouldn't be drinking himself into a stupor in the pub every evening. Besides, they'd all judged him already, anyway. He'd heard the whispers about why he was on the island. No doubt his sergeant had blackened his name before he'd even arrived.

Not that it mattered. Another five months and the whole pathetic scandal would have blown over. He'd be back in the Met, doing actual police work. In London, police officers were too busy keeping the peace to worry about what local residents thought of them.

Currently, there was no one around so he wasn't overly concerned about the fact that Melinda had just run her tongue along his ear lobe.

"What do you think?" she purred. "Shall I come over to your place later? Or you could come to my hotel..."

The easy excuse would be to say that he was working, which was partly true. Since he was the only healthy officer on the island, he was currently on call round the clock. But being on call didn't mean he couldn't socialise.

What else was he going to do with his evening? A night away from the Mermaid Inn might not be a bad thing. And he needed to find some pleasure while he killed the next five months on the island. There was no law that said police officers had to live like monks.

"Sounds good," he muttered, ignoring the twist of his gut and pushing down the part of him that was disgusted with himself. Not to mention the part which reminded him it was exactly this kind of situation which had got him a six-month posting on an island in the Atlantic.

Michaela lightly kissed the underside of his jaw, and the tickle made him turn his head away.

Across the road, a familiar face stared at him with a familiar judgemental glare. He should be used to people looking at him like that – the barmaid in the pub was particularly good at it – but there was something about the look on Lily's face that made his gut twist even further and increased the volume of the voice in his head which declared he was pathetic.

Still, he did nothing to move Melissa away from him. Instead, choosing to hold Lily's gaze and forcing his lips to a smirk. She could judge him all she wanted. He really didn't care.

Not one jot.

Subtly, he slipped a hand to Marissa's back and guided her to walk beside him.

"So," she said. "Your place or mine?"

He did his best to keep his features neutral. "I just remembered, I'm on duty tonight. My sergeant is ill, so I'm on call."

"So you'll be all alone at the station?" Her eyes darted to his. "I could come and keep you company…"

"Tempting as it is, I don't think that's a great idea."

She pouted. "It's fun to break the rules sometimes, isn't it?"

"Sometimes," he agreed. "But sometimes it gets you into more trouble than it's worth."

That he knew all too well.

Chapter Twenty-Six

OSCAR'S HOUSE was on the north-east corner of the island, meaning Lily got to walk a different path than she was used to. Not that the view was much different since she could still only see a few metres ahead. Stone walls ran alongside the narrow lane and beyond them green fields were just visible. Now and again, the verge would offer a smattering of wild flowers, but since Lily wasn't someone with a deep appreciation for the beauty of nature, she gave them little notice. Besides, she had too much on her mind to pay attention to her surroundings.

Nearing the house, she pondered what she'd say if faced with Oscar's parents, but her worries were unnecessary since she spotted him walking out of the house as she approached it.

He had his hood up and didn't spot her as he hurried along the lane ahead of her.

Lily called out to him, then broke into a run to catch up with him when he turned.

"What are you doing here?" He glanced around shiftily.

"Looking for you. I was worried about you after I saw you at the hotel."

"I'm fine," he said impatiently. "How did you even know

where I live?" He shook his head. "It doesn't even matter. I'm on my way to meet someone. I can't stop, I'm afraid."

"Wait." Lily put a hand on his arm to stop him. "I was worried about your friend, too. I got the impression Alanna might have upset her."

"I'll check on her, but I'm sure she's fine." Tugging his arm away, he set off at a brisk pace which Lily struggled to keep up with.

She wasn't sure what she was expecting to gain from following him, nor how long she intended to keep it up. Given the way he kept glancing back at her, she didn't think he'd put up with it for very long.

"What are you doing?" he asked, finally swinging around.

"I don't know." She fought off a laugh at her own terrible investigative skills. Covert operations clearly weren't her strong suit. She rubbed her hand across her forehead. If she was going to get to the bottom of what was going on, maybe the covert approach wasn't the best way to go about things, anyway. "I know about the camera," she blurted out.

He eyed her with a mix of distrust and suspicion. "What are you talking about?"

"I found Vinny's camera in the shed. I know it didn't just get lost. Someone took it."

"It was lost." He swallowed hard. "I found it in the garden this morning. Mr and Mrs Miller took it to the police."

"You're lying," she said. "Yesterday it was in the shed, not lost in the neighbour's garden."

"I don't know what you're talking about. I just found it in the neighbour's garden today."

She might have believed him, but he couldn't stand still and had guilt written all over his face.

"Look," she said, taking a softer tone. "I don't care that you stole the camera, but I need to know where the memory card is."

"What memory card?" His Adam's apple bobbed as he swallowed again.

"The one with the naked photos on it."

The fact that he didn't look surprised by the statement told Lily that he knew exactly what she was talking about.

"How do you know about that?" he asked.

"I found the camera in the shed yesterday and looked through the photos."

"Why were you even in the shed? No one goes in there except me."

"I told you; I was rescuing the cat..." She frowned, realising the implications of what Oscar had just said about being the only one to go in the shed. "You did steal the camera, then?"

"She only wanted the photos," he said meekly. "She changed her mind and just wanted them destroyed, but he wouldn't give them back. That's the only reason I took the camera – to get the photos." He paused and looked thoughtful. "And maybe to teach him a lesson."

"You need to slow down and explain this to me properly," Lily said. "Who wanted the photos?"

"Katie." He blew out a breath and glanced up and down the lane.

"The girl you were with at the house? The one who ran off in floods of tears today?"

"Yes."

"Wait." Lily squeezed her eyes closed, recalling the photos which she'd rather erase from her memory. "The photos were of Katie?"

"Yes."

"Why did Vinny have photos of Katie?" A wave of nausea swept through Lily as she thought of the look on the face of the girl in the photographs. So full of fear and vulnerability.

"He took them." Oscar glanced around again. "He offered her money and said the shots would be artistic and classy, but then he turned out to be a creep. He didn't pay her what he said he would and he threatened to put them all over the internet if she told anyone."

"So you stole his camera?"

"Yes," he said sheepishly. "Katie knew he was staying at the Miller's place, so she asked if I'd come with her to speak to him. She thought that if she had someone else with her, he might give her back the photos. But he just laughed at us." He sucked in a lungful of air. "The next day, I swiped his camera. I didn't even know for sure that the photos were on it, but I was so angry. I wanted to get back at him. So I stashed the camera in the shed and was going to throw it in the sea when I had a chance to sneak it away, but then he died." His voice switched to a low whisper. "I didn't know what to do then."

"But you handed it in to the police?"

"I was worried how it would look if someone caught me moving it. There'd be a lot of questions."

"Yeah." He was right about that. "So what did you do with the memory card?"

"How do you mean?"

"I mean where is the memory card now?" She tilted her head. "What Vinny did was wrong, and the police should know about it."

"They do know," he said. "I handed the memory card in with the camera. It was in a pocket in the camera case. I shouldn't have, because I told Katie I'd give her the memory card. She's going to kill me when she finds out I handed it in. "

"That doesn't make sense," Lily said as her mind whirred. "The police don't have the memory card."

"They might not have seen it yet, but when they properly look through the camera case, they'll find the extra memory cards."

"They already did," she said. "But the one with the photos of Katie wasn't there."

"How do you know?"

"Because I was at the police station this morning, and I looked through the camera case with PC Grainger."

His eyes widened. "Are you sure it wasn't there?"

"Certain."

He released a relieved breath. "That's good."

"Why is it good?" Lily asked. "And where is the memory card now?"

"It's good because Katie doesn't want anyone to know about the photos. But I don't know where the memory card could be..." He looked thoughtful. "I'm sure I put it back in the camera case. At least, I think it was there... I thought I checked it... but I was also panicking about getting caught. Maybe I dropped it."

Lily rubbed her hand across her forehead. "Without the memory card, the police won't investigate further..."

"You want them to investigate the photographs?" Oscar's words were slow, cautious.

She shook her head. "I want them to investigate Vinny's death."

"But he just fell," Oscar said, eyes narrowing. "Him being a pervert doesn't make his death suspicious, does it?"

"Not according to PC Grainger."

Oscar's shoulders relaxed and he pulled his phone from his pocket to respond to a message. "I have to go," he told Lily. "Katie's waiting for me. She was ignoring my calls after Vinny died, but suddenly she's desperate to talk. I'm on my way to her place."

"Can I come?" Lily asked.

"I don't think she'd like it. She's been pretty shaken up since Vinny did his so-called photo shoot. She's terrified of people finding out about it. You can't mention it to anyone."

"Maybe she'd like to speak to another woman about it," Lily ventured. "It must be hard for her to keep it to herself. I might be able to help."

If he said no, she suspected she'd follow him anyway. Perhaps he suspected the same, as he gave a noncommittal shrug and led the way.

Chapter Twenty-Seven

"WHAT'S GOING ON?" Katie asked, not opening the front door fully.

"Lily asked if she could come too," Oscar said.

Katie's nose wrinkled. "You're staying at the B&B." It was more of a statement than a question.

"She knows about the photos," Oscar whispered.

Katie looked as though she might be about to close the door in their faces. "Why?"

"She found the camera in the shed."

"I thought maybe I could help." Lily offered what she hoped was a reassuring smile, but wasn't convinced she'd hit her mark.

"I said not to tell anyone," Katie hissed at Oscar.

"I didn't," he shot back. "She already knew."

"Clearly Vinny was awful," Lily said, attempting to present herself as an ally. "I can't believe he used you like that."

Katie's features softened. "He showed me these arty black and white photos. In those photos you couldn't see any of the women's private parts, or their faces. And he offered me a lot of money..." She pressed her lips together, then met Lily's gaze.

"It wasn't like that when he took my photo. I realised quickly, but not quickly enough. He'd already taken a bunch of pictures."

"Can we come in?" Oscar asked.

Reluctantly, Katie opened the door wider and stepped aside to reveal a long hallway. "My parents will be out for an hour or so."

"What did you want to tell me about?" Oscar asked as they entered the large kitchen at the back of the house. "You said you'd found something out..."

"Yes." Her eyes brightened as she sank into a chair at the solid wooden table. In front of her, a laptop was already open. "It wasn't just me," she said as she clicked on the keypad. "I've been talking to a woman online and Vinny did the same thing to her. Promised her artistic shots and then took seedy ones. Then he refused to pay her."

The chairs scraped on the stone tiles as Lily and Oscar sat on either side of Katie.

"How did you find her?" Lily asked.

"I was doing some digging around, checking Vinny's social media sites and stuff. At first I was panicking, thinking he might post photos of me somewhere." She gave a quick shake of the head. "Now, I realise that was stupid. He wouldn't post them where anyone could see them. He'd get himself into trouble that way, wouldn't he?" The innocence in her wide eyes made Lily's heart squeeze as she looked questioningly at her. She nodded in response.

"Anyway," Katie went on. "The only official work of his I could find was the photography he does..." She caught herself and grimaced. "The only work he *did* was the stuff for Alanna Harding. It seemed weird that a photographer wouldn't have more clients or jobs, but I guess she kept him busy." She frowned as though she'd lost her train of thought, then she gave a quick shake of her head and continued. "I saw Alanna write a post about his death and I got a bit obsessed by the comment section. Lots of people were sympathetic and shocked... but some of them..."

Lily's eyelids popped. "Some of the women were glad he's dead."

"Did you see the comments, too?" Katie asked.

"No, but someone in the pub mentioned it."

"I saw a few women make similar remarks," Katie said. "Alanna must have been monitoring it because the comments would disappear. But I messaged one of them before Alanna could hide the comment." She swivelled the laptop in Lily's direction. "We've been messaging, and she told me how Vinny had done exactly the same to her about a year ago."

"Wow." Lily's eyes scanned the emotionally charged exchange between the two women.

"She says she wanted to go to the police but was worried about her job. She was worried it would look bad if it came out that she'd posed naked for money."

"I wonder how many times he did it," Lily mused.

"Probably a lot," Katie said, her eyes fixed on Lily. "I know it's stupid, but it makes me feel better that it wasn't just me. I felt like such an idiot for believing what he told me, but now it kind of feels as though it wasn't my fault."

"Of course it wasn't," Lily said. "He was a sicko and he exploited you."

"I should never have agreed to him taking my photos, no matter how badly I wanted the money."

"What you agreed to do for the money and what happened were two different things," Lily pointed out. "How did you meet him, anyway?"

"Alanna was doing a photo shoot a couple of weeks ago, over on Tresco. I went with a few friends to hang out and see if we could get a photo with her." She shrugged. "Alanna was sweet in a fake kind of way. She seemed to like that she had people coming to watch her. She made a bit of a fuss of us and chatted to us for a while."

Her eyes misted over. "I got chatting to Vinny and he said I had great looks for modelling. It sounds stupid now, but he seemed genuine. He told me he was working on a project that he thought I'd be perfect for. He had this folder with examples of the other photo shoots he'd done. At first I was surprised that the models were naked, but like I said, it all looked really classy and artful. I wasn't going to agree to it, but then he mentioned the money. Also, the way he talked about the models and the nudity made me feel at ease with it all."

"Where did you do the photo shoot?" Lily asked.

"He was staying in a holiday cottage on Tresco. I went over there." Her lips twitched. "I was a complete idiot."

"No." Lily shook her head. "He's the problem, not you."

"He's not really a problem, any more," Oscar pointed out.

"The police didn't listen to me when I told them about the photos," Lily said. "But I'm sure they'd listen to you. Especially now that you've found someone else with the same experience."

Katie's eyes widened. "You went to the police?"

"I didn't know the photos were of you," she said. "I didn't look closely and I'd only seen you once anyway. But it seemed like something the police should know about."

"And they didn't listen?"

Lily thought back on PC Grainger's initial reaction. He *had* listened. He'd believed her. But in a few hours he'd changed his tune considerably.

"They need proof," she said, choosing to believe that was the only issue. "That's all. I didn't have the memory card, and without that, there wasn't much to investigate. Especially since I didn't know who the photos were of."

"I can't go to the police," Katie said, looking desperately at Oscar. "I *can't*. And he's dead now, so there isn't even any point."

Oscar shrugged in noncommittal agreement.

Part of Lily wanted to agree. Clearly, Katie wanted to put

the whole thing behind her, and a police investigation was the opposite of that. But...

"There's a chance Vinny was just taking the photos for his own sick entertainment," she said slowly. "But what if there was more to it?"

"Like he was selling them?" Katie asked.

"Yes."

"He can't sell photos of me when he's dead, can he?"

Lily bobbed her head ambiguously. "There are also the other women he's done this to."

"But he'll already have sold any photos he was going to. Exposing him won't stop that now. I really don't see the point. It won't help anything; it'll just cause a lot of problems for me."

"What kind of problems?" Lily asked.

Katie choked on a humourless laugh. "Are you serious? You really think I want my parents knowing that I let a guy photograph me naked for money? You think I want *anyone* knowing that?"

"Okay, your parents might find out about it," Lily conceded. "But there's such a thing as confidentiality. The police won't advertise what happened to you."

"I'm not going to the police," she said firmly. "No way. There's not even any point."

"I don't think you understand," Lily said. "It's not as though pornography is sold as a one-time deal. He could have already uploaded your photos somewhere for some sickos to access."

Katie paled. "What?"

"Yes." Lily felt a rush of annoyance by how naïve Katie was. "If he was sick enough to take photos of vulnerable young women, he's sick enough to do a lot more."

"Oh, god." Katie buried her face in her hands.

"Let the police investigate it," Lily said, resting a reassuring hand on Katie's shoulder.

"It feels like a bad idea." When she removed her hands from her face, she looked at Oscar for support.

Lily waited for Oscar to encourage her and felt a tightening in her gut when he shook his head.

"It might cause more issues," he said evenly. "Maybe it's better to just put it behind you. The guy's dead and I really don't think he'd have had time to do anything with your photos."

"And what about the other women?" Lily asked.

"Why should Katie be responsible for them?" Oscar snapped. "If they want to report him, they can." He took Katie's hand and squeezed it. "This has been hard enough for you already. I don't want to watch you go through more stress."

"Thank you," Katie said, leaning towards Oscar and slipping her arms around his waist. "Did you bring the memory card?"

"No," he said, avoiding eye contact with Lily. "I hid it."

"You didn't look at the photos, did you?"

His cheek twitched. "No."

"Promise me you won't."

"I won't."

Lily decided not to reveal that he was lying through his teeth. At least about hiding the memory card. She suspected he was also lying about not having looked at the photos.

Her mind drifted back to seeing Katie at the house that morning. "Did you speak to Alanna about this?"

"Yes." Katie rested her head on Oscar's shoulder. "I told her everything this morning, after I'd been talking to this woman online, but Alanna just had a go at me. She said he was dead, and he was a nice guy and that I shouldn't go around saying awful things about him when he's dead. She thinks I'm attention-seeking."

Lily raised an eyebrow, thinking of the tone of Alanna's social media posts. "That seems quite hypocritical," she said quietly.

"That's another reason I shouldn't go to the police. If she thinks that, other people will say the same. It's my word against a dead guy's."

"Not really," Lily said. "Somewhere there'll be proof of all of this. For a start, there's the woman you were speaking to online. You already know you're not alone in this."

"I'll think about it," Katie said, but Lily got the impression she was only saying it to put an end to the conversation.

She didn't seem keen for them to hang around much longer, panicking about her parents arriving home. Not that Lily was upset about being rushed out of the door.

"We have to find that memory card before anyone else does," Oscar said as soon as they'd left.

Lily nodded. "I was thinking the same thing."

Though she was fairly sure they had different motives for wanting to find it. *She* wanted it handed to the police so they might finally take action. Whereas she suspected Oscar wanted to hand it over to Katie to gain brownie points with her.

Which meant she'd really like to find it before he did.

Chapter Twenty Eight

MAYBE IT WAS because the investigative part of Lily's brain was in overdrive, but when they reached the house and Oscar told her to wait outside while he searched the shed, it set alarm bells ringing.

"I'll come and help you look," she said, following him down the side of the house.

"Okay. You check the garden while I look in the shed."

Lily felt frown lines crease her forehead. "Do you really not know where it is?"

"What?" His eyes bounced from his feet to Lily's face and back again. "I told you, I thought I'd handed it in, but I was stressed. I might have dropped it."

"Or you might have kept it for yourself," she suggested.

"Why would I do that?"

Lily rolled her eyes. "Why would you keep a memory card full of naked photos?"

"She's my friend," he said angrily. "I wouldn't do that."

"Oh, yeah. You're so gallant that you didn't even look at them, right?"

A patch of red spread up his neck. "I promised Katie I wouldn't look at them, and I didn't. We just need to find the memory card so I can give it to her." Turning his back on Lily, he opened the shed.

"I think we should give it to the police," Lily said, following him into the dreary space. "That was your intention before, wasn't it?"

"Yes, but now I realise it should be Katie's decision." He moved plant pots aside as he searched the shelves. "If she doesn't want the police to investigate it, that's up to her."

When a thorough search of the shed revealed nothing, Oscar pointed Lily to the area of the garden she should search. He claimed he didn't want the Millers to see him in the garden when he wasn't supposed to be at work.

Lily couldn't help but think that the reason he wasn't helping to search was because he knew it would be fruitless. It didn't seem believable that the memory card just got lost somewhere, and she couldn't come up with any logical conclusion other than him having taken it for some evening entertainment.

The thought made Lily's stomach churn. How anyone could take pleasure from the photos was beyond her. You'd really need to have some sick fantasies. Oscar seemed like a decent kid, but he was also a hormone-riddled teenager. Likely with a massive crush on Katie.

As she expected, the search of the garden was fruitless, and she indicated as much to Oscar with a shake of her head when she wandered back towards the shed.

"I don't understand," he said. "I really don't know what happened to it."

As she watched him leave, Lily really wished she believed that statement. As things stood, she could only think that Oscar must have the memory card.

At least she knew who the photos were of now. Maybe that information would be enough to get the police to take notice. But not if Katie refused to speak to them.

Oscar was right that it needed to be her decision.

Which meant Lily was firmly back to square one.

"You look very serious." Mrs Miller's voice startled Lily when she walked inside. With her mind desperately chewing over the events of the last few hours, she hadn't noticed Flora in the hallway.

Lily shot her a questioning look. It wasn't that she hadn't heard her words – she just wasn't sure how to respond.

"You look as though you have the weight of the world on your shoulders. Is everything okay?"

Her instinct was to insist she was fine, but she stopped herself before the words came. Because she wasn't okay. She *did* feel as though she had the weight of the world on her shoulders. Maybe not the world, but a heavy burden. And she shouldn't have to bear it alone. In fact, she shouldn't have to bear it at all. The police should be investigating.

Thinking back on PC Grainger's dismissal of her concerns, she was suddenly furious.

"Does it strike you as odd that the police aren't looking more closely into Vinny's death?" she blurted out.

The question seemed to shock Mrs Miller so much that she physically tensed. "How do you mean?"

"I mean they quickly assumed it was an accident without looking into it. I can't help but think they should investigate more thoroughly."

"Why would they need to?" Mrs Miller asked, gathering her composure and standing ramrod straight. "The poor man fell. What's to investigate?"

"Maybe he didn't just fall," Lily stated. "Maybe there was someone else with him."

Red heat crept up Mrs Miller's neck, then turned her cheeks a fiery shade too. "What an outrageous allegation," she spat, a sudden fury in her eyes that Lily wouldn't have thought her capable of. "It's absurd, and I can tell you exactly why the police didn't follow that line of enquiry... because it would turn a heartbreaking tragedy into a circus. I imagine his poor family is suffering enough without a bunch of wild stories flying around. Why would you even think of that?"

There was a whole list of reasons that she didn't care to get into, but there was also one very basic piece of information which no one was talking about.

"He was a physically fit young man. I realise it was foggy, but that makes it even more strange that he'd be hanging around at the edge of a cliff. But also, the cliff wasn't *that* high. If he just slipped off the edge, he should have been able to at least break his fall."

Mrs Miller pushed her fidgeting hands over the front of her blouse. "Those rocks are treacherous after the rain. Have you ever tried walking over wet, slippery rocks?"

Lily thought back on all the times she'd spent exploring rock pools as a kid. "Yes," she said flatly. "Lots of times. It just never occurred to me that wet rocks would be considered deadly terrain. Mostly because people aren't usually stupid enough to walk on wet rocks on the precipice of a cliff."

"What a disrespectful way to speak about the deceased," Mrs Miller huffed. "Sometimes tragic accidents happen. That's a fact of life." With her nose in the air, she stalked away before Lily could question which scenario it was: a tragic accident, or an inevitable occurrence on treacherous rocks. Because she'd flicked from one argument to another incredibly quickly.

Why had she been so defensive, anyway?

Chapter Twenty-Nine

WEDNESDAY

AFTER ANOTHER NIGHT of disturbed sleep, Lily woke feeling defeated. Yesterday's investigative attempts had provided more questions than answers, and at some point in the night she'd become entirely frustrated with herself for spending so much mental energy on it.

If the police didn't deem it worth their time, why was she so determined to look into it?

Deep down, she knew the answer. It was the same reason she'd spent the last six months searching for an ice cream shop. She needed to keep her mind occupied to keep her from dwelling on the fact that she was all alone in the world with no idea what to do with her life.

Making a plan for her life would be a more sensible use of her time. Or she could use her remaining time on the island for a holiday. She could spend a few days relaxing and then go back to Truro and find herself a job to give some structure to her life.

The idea of a holiday didn't spur any warm feelings. Especially when she pulled the curtains back and took in the thick fog which remained, hanging in the air like industrial smog. In a place renowned for its natural beauty, the weather made it difficult to get out and take in the sights.

Her phone pinged with a notification and she sank back on the bed as she opened her email. She'd signed up to Alanna's blog and had a notification about a new post. Idly, she clicked the link.

Her shoulders tensed as she read the title: **Heartbreak of Vinny's Final Photographs.** It went on to describe how upsetting it had been for Alanna to look through Vinny's most recent photos on his camera. She'd uploaded a selection. Lily cringed as she peered at the ones she'd chosen to share. All of Alanna. Given the circumstances, she could probably have chosen some scenes of nature, but apparently that hadn't occurred to her.

Looking again, Lily realised she'd seen some of the photos before. When she'd found the camera in the shed. Which meant...

With a quick shake of her head, Lily went back to read the blog post again. It stated that Alanna had 'the heartbreaking task' of poring over Vinny's camera the previous day.

When would she have had access to his camera? Oscar had found it and handed it to the Millers, who had passed it to the police. Had PC Grainger returned it to Alanna? He'd said it would be given to Vinny's sister with the rest of his things, but maybe he'd let Alanna have it. It seemed like an odd move, but then again so did not investigating his death properly.

Lily stretched her neck, contemplating. Maybe she should leave it alone. Even with the miserable weather, she should be able to find something to do that didn't involve tying herself in knots trying to make sense of a situation that only made her more confused at every turn.

Her stomach rumbled, giving her the nudge she needed to

get moving and go in search of food. When her conversation with Mrs Miller came back to her, she decided finding breakfast elsewhere would probably be a good idea.

Sadly, her attempt to slip out of the house unnoticed didn't quite work out. Mrs Miller seemed to be waiting for her and popped out of the breakfast room as soon as her foot hit the stairs.

"Good morning," she said, a slight quiver in her voice.

"Morning," Lily replied with a polite smile. "I don't need breakfast today, thank you."

Mrs Miller didn't respond until Lily reached the foot of the stairs. "I don't blame you," she said quietly. "But if you have a moment, I would like to speak to you."

"I was just heading out," Lily said.

"Please." Mrs Miller tipped her head towards the living room. "I won't keep you for long."

With an impatient sigh, Lily changed course. As she passed the breakfast room, she spotted Marc sitting alone with a coffee in front of him. He looked up from his phone to give her a friendly smile.

In the living room, Mrs Miller closed the door behind them and Lily perched on the edge of the sofa.

"I wanted to apologise for yesterday," Flora said.

"Okay," Lily replied.

"I feel terrible." Flora sank onto the arm of the couch. "I snapped at you and I shouldn't have done. I barely slept for thinking about how rude I was."

"I think we're all a bit on edge at the moment."

Flora managed a weak smile. "The weather isn't helping. Being cooped up isn't good for anyone."

"I'm sure it will clear soon," Lily said.

"About that," Flora said. "According to the weather forecast, the fog should lift overnight tonight. I know our other guests are keen to leave as soon as possible, so I just wanted to check that you're still planning to stay until Friday?"

"Yes," Lily said slowly. "Is that a problem?"

"No, no," Flora said quickly. "It's not a problem at all. It's only that I've been desperate to see my daughter. I've booked myself and my husband on the ferry tomorrow morning. You'll be here alone for your final night, but I've asked my neighbour to pop in and cook your breakfast. And if there's anything else you need, I'll leave her number. That wouldn't be a problem for you, would it?"

"No." Having the place to herself sounded like absolute bliss. "That's fine."

"Perfect. That's all I wanted to tell you. And I'm sorry again for yesterday. I wasn't myself."

"Really, it's fine." Lily couldn't ignore the look of despair in Mrs Miller's features. "Are you okay?" she asked, giving the words the weight of a genuine enquiry rather than a polite nicety.

Mrs Miller wrung her hands in front of her. "My nerves are a little fraught, that's all. I'm sure some time away is all I need." She paused and caught Lily's eye. "I'm concerned about my husband, too. He's been out of sorts recently. You weren't there, but he shouted at Mr Roth the other day. It was so unlike him. It was like something snapped inside him."

Lily thought back, trying to recall the incident which she'd secretly watched from her window. Given the way Vinny had provoked him, she actually thought Mr Miller had been quite controlled.

"That's why I got so upset yesterday when you suggested the police should investigate further," Flora added.

"Why would that bother you?"

She shrugged. "If they ask more questions, it will come out that Rodney had argued with Mr Roth. It might look bad, I suppose."

"But..." Lily frowned, stunned by the turn of the conversation. "You don't think..."

"No," Flora said quickly, before a flash of uncertainty hit

her eyes. "No." More firmly this time. "Of course not. It's only that he was embarrassed about losing his temper, so I'd hate for him to have to relive it and have to answer police questions about it."

"It's normal that people lose their temper from time to time. I'm sure they'd see it for what it was." Another thought struck her. "He was here in the house with you when Vinny died, so it's not as though anyone could accuse him of anything."

"Yes," Mrs Miller said, the uncertainty returning to her voice. "We were together."

Lily's heart rate increased as she eyed Flora intently. "He *was* with you, wasn't he? You sound as though you're not sure."

"He was here." She nodded firmly but didn't meet Lily's eye. "Here with me the whole time." The smile she gave Lily looked entirely forced. "Are you sure you don't want breakfast?" she asked, her tone overly sunny.

"No, thank you."

After watching Flora scuttle back to the breakfast room, Lily ventured to the front door with her mind whirring even more than it had been before.

Chapter Thirty

IF SHE WAS the suspicious type, Lily would swear there'd been something fishy about her conversation with Mrs Miller. And if she wanted to investigate the matter further, she'd definitely take a closer look at where exactly Mr Miller was at the time of Vinny's death. It wouldn't surprise her to find he wasn't where he said he'd been. Not given how cagey Mrs Miller had looked when questioned about it.

But Lily wasn't the suspicious type, and she wasn't investigating anything. What she was going to do, she decided as she walked out of the house, was visit PC Grainger and fill him in on what she'd learned. If the information she'd gleaned was worth investigating further, he could handle it. If not, then she'd done all she could. From then on, she was going to focus on enjoying a little holiday.

A figure in her peripheral made her look up.

"Hi," she said to Alanna, who was perched on the stone wall by the garden gate. For the first time since Lily had met her, the emotion in her features looked genuine. "Are you okay?"

She nodded in reply. "I just went for a little walk. It got me thinking about Vinny going out for a walk and having no clue it was the last thing he'd do."

Lily's instinct was to engage Alanna in conversation. Why though? She'd decided she was going to leave the investigating alone and focus on having a holiday, so she really shouldn't keep probing.

"I guess you and Vinny must have been close?" she asked, cursing her lack of self-control. "You worked together for quite a while, didn't you?"

"Yes." She looked away. That would be a good time for Lily to walk away. She looked along the lane, contemplating exactly that. "We didn't always get on, though," Alanna added quietly.

"I don't think many people get on with their colleagues all the time," Lily said. "And you were travelling together, so it must have been pretty intense."

"It was. In the last six months we'd been arguing a lot." She took a shuddering breath. "It'll sound awful, but a couple of times since he died, I've thought..." Pausing, she sniffed and pulled a tissue from her pocket. "Sometimes I've thought it's almost a relief. That makes me an awful person, doesn't it?"

For lack of an answer, Lily shrugged. "You can't help how you feel."

"He was a brilliant photographer," she said. "And I knew him since we were kids. You know how there are some people who you're friends with purely because you've known them so long?"

No, not at all. To be agreeable, Lily gave a quick nod.

"He was fun when we were younger, but he didn't want to grow up. In the end, he was starting to feel like a liability."

"In what way?"

Alanna tipped her head from side to side. "He had a thing for younger women. Nothing illegal or anything, but he was thirty, and still chasing eighteen-year-olds. He could charm them," she said nonchalantly. "But he was mostly using them.

We travelled a lot, which was advantageous for him. He'd hook up with some woman, and they were always young and naïve enough to think it was more than it was. He left a trail of broken hearts, and mostly left me to deal with the aftermath."

"What kind of aftermath?" Lily asked, taking a step closer to Alanna.

"The women would get angry, of course. And when he ignored them, they'd pop up on my blog, saying what they thought of him there."

Lily pushed a lock of hair behind her ear. "I saw someone had commented something nasty when you posted that he'd died."

"Horrible, isn't it? They won't stop even now he's dead. There are a few women who troll my blog and write something horrible every time I post. That's what I argued with Vinny over. I couldn't cope with the negativity and I didn't want to work with him any more."

"I don't blame you. It sounds very unprofessional."

"I know it sounds daft, but that blog is my baby. I'm actually good at it," she said tearfully. "I grew up being told I'd never amount to anything and I've created a thriving business from nothing."

"That's something to be proud of." Lily tried not to dwell on what lengths a person might go to in order to protect the life they loved. "I saw you posted more photos this morning," she said, redirecting the conversation. "They were really great."

"He was a talented photographer," Alanna said firmly. "It was heartbreaking to go through his most recent photos, but it also felt soothing in a way. Like a part of him was still alive. I just wish he knew the camera hadn't been stolen, only lost. He was furious when he thought someone had taken it."

"Were the photos you posted ones you found on the camera?" Lily asked, pretending she hadn't read the blog post, which stated exactly that.

"Yes. I was so happy when Mrs Miller told me they'd found the camera."

"It must have been a relief." Lily took a breath while deciding the best way to find out what she wanted to know. "I thought the Millers handed it to the police," she said as casually as she could manage. "Did the police give it back to you?"

"No. Mrs Miller let me have a look before they handed it in so I downloaded the photos from it."

Lily's whole body seemed to buzz at the new information. It meant that Alanna could easily have taken the memory card.

"The police will give all Vinny's belongings to his sister," Alanna said. "Once they finally track her down. Except—" The sound of the door opening behind them cut her off and she turned to smile at Marc.

"Your breakfast is ready," he said with a sympathetic smile. "Do you feel like eating?"

"Not really, but I should have something." She straightened up, then gave Lily's arm a pat as she passed her. "Enjoy your day, and the rest of your holiday, if we don't see you later. It looks as though we'll be leaving in the morning."

"Take care," Lily said as the front door closed behind them, leaving her wondering what Alanna had been about to say. She rubbed at her temples and tried not to let her brain get caught up with dissecting everything Alanna had said. Just as with everything else she'd found, she'd let PC Grainger know, and then it was off her plate for good.

Her phone rang just as she set off down the lane. Seeing the unknown number flash on the screen, she hesitated over answering it. At the last minute, she realised it might have been the solicitor, Mr Greaves, but she'd already missed the call.

It turned out not to be him, anyway. A message popped up immediately. It was Kit, who'd got her number from Seren. Apparently, his mum remembered the owner of the ice cream shop and would be happy to talk to her if she was still interested. He included his mum's address and phone number, and said she was always happy to have visitors if Lily wanted to call by. Excitedly, Lily tapped out a message expressing her gratitude. She pondered the idea of calling his mum, but decided an in-person conversation would be easier.

She'd pay her a visit and then she'd visit PC Grainger.

After that, she was officially in holiday mode.

Chapter Thirty One

At Old Town Lily could make out a couple of boats bobbing in the bay. A misty haze lingered in the air, but it seemed the weather forecast was right that the fog was lifting. If it turned out to be a clear day tomorrow, she could get out and see the sights and enjoy her last day on the island before she went back to establish some kind of real life.

Stopping at the end of the quiet lane, Lily gazed out over the horseshoe beach and the peaceful bay.

Real life: what did that even mean? She'd be back at her rented flat in Truro, and was sure that finding a job would be a good move. Was that enough though? Was it really a life she wanted?

She shook the thoughts from her head, deciding to focus on the task in front of her for now.

Sucking in a lungful of salty air, she turned to the gate beside her. The sign read 'Treneary House', so she was certain she had the right place. There was no bell, so she unlatched the gate and set off slowly along the path to the house which loomed up on the headland.

"Hello!" a sing-song voice called out to her as she

approached. An angelic-looking little girl swung her hips, making her flowy skirt sweep around her knees.

"Hi," Lily said, glancing behind the girl, searching for an adult.

"Are you Mirren's friend?" The girl was probably around six or seven and eyed Lily with open curiosity.

"I don't know her," Lily said. "But I am looking for her."

She giggled. "Why are you looking for her if you don't know her?"

Again, Lily glanced behind the child, assuming an adult would appear at any moment. "I just wanted to ask her something. Her son told me she might be able to help me..."

"She has five sons," the girl said.

"Oh." Lily gave a small smile. "It was Kit."

"Kit is very nice. He drives the train and he taught me to swim and he's very funny. Trystan is my daddy."

"Right," Lily said, maintaining her weak smile. "Is Mirren here?"

"Yes. She's my granny."

Lily shifted her weight. "Do you think you could get her?"

"She's putting my brother in bed for his nap. He's just a baby and he cries when he gets tired. He was crying a lot today."

"I see. Maybe I should come back later."

"It's okay. You can come in and wait. My name is Ellie. Do you want to be my friend?"

Lily gazed down at her, thinking that someone needed to teach the child a thing or two about safety. "You shouldn't invite people into your house if you don't know them."

"But you know Kit," Ellie said, "so it's okay."

Lily opened her mouth to argue, but movement in the house caught her attention. A face peered through the window and the older lady waved, then came to the door.

"Hello!" she said, apparently unconcerned that her granddaughter was chatting to a stranger on the doorstep. "Sorry, I was just settling my grandson for his nap."

"This lady is Kit's friend," Ellie said.

"Lily, I assume?" The woman extended her hand. "I'm Mirren. Kit said you might call in." Stepping back, she beckoned Lily inside. "I was just about to make myself a cuppa. Would you like one?"

"Yes, please." As Lily followed Mirren into the large, homely kitchen, Ellie kept her unwavering gaze on her.

"Do you want to see my toys?" she asked. "I have lots."

"Umm..."

Mirren placed a hand on Ellie's head. "Lily has come to speak to me, not to play. And you're supposed to be clearing up the living room so you can have TV time, remember?"

She looked thoughtful before agreeing and heading out of the kitchen.

"She's a sweet little thing," Mirren remarked. "Had a tummy ache this morning so she couldn't go to school but she seems as right as rain now. I think she just knew I was having her brother for the day and wanted to spend the day here too."

Lily smiled amiably and took a seat at the table when Mirren nodded in that direction.

"So you're interested in the old ice cream shop?" she asked, once she'd filled the kettle and switched it on.

"Yes. I'm interested in the owner. Do you remember her name, by any chance?"

Mirren took a seat. "Gail. It's funny, I haven't thought about her in ages, but when Kit told me you'd been asking about her, it stirred my memory."

Gail. The name didn't stir any memories for Lily.

"Did you know her well?"

"Pretty well. My kids were still young at that time so I spent a fair bit of time in the ice cream shop."

"Were you friends with her?"

Mirren frowned. "I wouldn't say that. She was always

171

lovely and friendly... and I guess we were around the same age. We were at different phases of life, though. She was focussed on her business and I was chasing around after my kids."

"Do you know her surname?"

"It's going to annoy me." Mirren rubbed at her forehead. "It'll come back to me in a minute, I'm sure."

Lily wasn't convinced Mirren was going to prove overly helpful. She had a first name at least, so that was something.

"How long did Gail live on the island for?"

"Not too long. A few years, I think. She was one of those who turned up with a dream of living remotely and being her own boss. If I remember rightly, she'd worked in an ice cream shop when she was a teenager and had always dreamed of having her own shop. Finally, she gave up the drudgery of her office job and moved here."

"But it didn't work out?"

"As far as I know, things were going well for her. She never gave any indication that there were problems with the business. She made ice cream fresh on the premises and was hardly ever short on customers."

"Do you know why she left?"

Mirren shook her head. "I remember she was out of sorts for a couple of months and then there was the fire. That shook her up. People pitched in to help fix the place up again, but she'd lost her spark. Her heart didn't seem to be in it after that. To my recollection, she shut up shop one day and left without saying goodbye to anyone. It was all a bit odd."

It was certainly intriguing. "You said she was out of sorts?" Lily pressed.

"I think she was having some personal problems. Someone died... I can't remember if it was a family member or an old friend... but I remember it really got to her. I thought it was just one of those things and it would take time for her to bounce back, but then she was gone." She shrugged. "Kit reckons she never sold the shop, and that she still owns it." Her eyes widened and she snapped her fingers loudly. "Greenway! That was her last name."

As though the name might be forgotten again, Lily hurriedly opened her phone and made a note of it. "Gail Greenway," she mused, hoping it might spark a memory, but nothing came.

"Do you know her?" Mirren asked.

"No. I don't think so." She drew the old photograph from her pocket and handed it to Mirren. "This is me and my parents."

"In front of the ice cream shop," Mirren mused.

"Yes. I have a feeling Gail might have been the one to take the photo." She paused, feeling an unexpected pang of sadness. "My parents both died, probably not long after this photo was taken. I only found the photo recently, and..." She paused again. "I'm probably being silly and nostalgic, but I have this strange feeling that the ice cream shop was somehow meaningful... like my parents were friends with the owner or something." She felt even more emotional at the sympathy in Mirren's eyes. "I spent ages tracking down the ice cream shop. It feels a bit deflating that I couldn't track down the owner, but now that I know her name I might have more luck. Maybe I can find her on the internet."

"Maybe." Mirren patted her hand. "I'm sorry I can't be more helpful."

"It's a massive help to have her name. That should be helpful in tracking her down." Except, she was supposed to be giving all this up and figuring out what to do with her life.

She could allow herself a simple internet search, though. What harm could that do?

Chapter Thirty-Two

THE PATCHY INTERNET signal meant Lily would have to wait until later to see what she could find out about Gail Greenway. After so many months of searching, having a name felt significant. She just wished the name meant something to her, but it didn't jog her memory in the slightest.

After strolling through Hugh Town, Lily arrived at the police station and stepped quietly inside. "Are you still working alone?" she asked PC Grainger, who was sitting in the same spot he'd been the last time she'd been there. An image of him and his blonde friend popped into her head, and she shoved it aside.

"The sergeant and PC Hill are still ill," he told her.

She nodded, trying not to convey her disappointment. Maybe if the sergeant had been there, he might take her concerns more seriously. As it was, she'd once again have to convince PC Grainger, and she suspected she was starting out on uneven ground. Not that it mattered. All she had to do was pass on what she'd uncovered and then it was out of her hands.

"What can I help you with today?" The way he stressed the word *today* made it sound as though she was a nuisance he had to deal with regularly.

She sat heavily on the chair opposite him. "I know you said you wouldn't look any further into Vinny's death, but I wanted to update you on what I've found... in case it might make you reconsider."

He sighed as he rested his elbows on the table. "You've been playing Miss Marple, have you?"

She shrugged. "I see myself as more of a modern detective. And younger than Marple, obviously, but I see what you're getting at. And yes, I have been digging into the incident, but it was hard not to."

"Really? I know the weather hasn't been brilliant, but I'm sure you could have found something else to entertain yourself. If hiking isn't your thing, there's always Netflix... surely you have Netflix?"

"I..." She opened and closed her mouth repeatedly. The mocking in his tone scrambled her carefully constructed thoughts into chaos. Taking a steady breath, she vowed not to let him goad her. "I'm only here to report what I've found," she said archly.

"Fine." He leaned back in his chair and interlocked his fingers on his chest. "Hit me with it."

"Well." She swallowed hard, annoyed with herself for getting flustered. The more confident and arrogant he was, the more feeble she felt. "I don't know who did it," she said.

"Who did what?"

"Killed Vinny."

"Right," he said, raising an eyebrow. "Of course. That's helpful."

"I can't even say for certain that someone did," she said, choosing to ignore his teasing. "There's definitely some stuff that seems dodgy."

"Such as?"

"I'm fairly sure he was involved in some criminal activity. Specifically pornography." She cut him off when he tried to speak. "Before you ask, no, I didn't find the memory card, but I found the subject of the photos." She described her visit to Katie and the fact that at least one other woman had experienced the same.

"If Katie doesn't want to make a statement, I can't really follow it up."

"I'm hoping she might change her mind."

PC Grainger leaned forwards. "You mentioned that you think someone killed Mr Roth. Are you suggesting that Katie pushed him off the cliff?"

"She has a motive," Lily mused, though she couldn't really see Katie doing it. "But I think Oscar might be in love with Katie, which also gives him a motive. I also wonder if he has the missing memory card."

"Any other suspects?"

"Yes." She tapped on the desk. "I get the impression that Mrs Miller is covering for Mr Miller. I don't think they were actually together at the time of Vinny's death. Also, Flora said she's been worried about her husband's mental state. She said it was out of character for him to have a go at Vinny the way he did. Plus, they're making a last-minute trip to the mainland tomorrow. That seems fishy to me."

"Okay," PC Grainger said.

"There's also Alanna Harding to consider. She confided in me that she was relieved Vinny was dead. Apparently, she'd been trying to nudge him out of her business for a while. She called him a liability." Lily frowned. "I suppose that also makes her boyfriend a suspect since he'd probably be protective of her."

She paused when she noticed her words were tumbling out in a rush, but there was more she had to say. "Also, I can't figure out the missing memory card. I don't know who took it or why? At first I thought it was Oscar, but now I wonder if it was Alanna. She's concerned about her blog, and it would definitely reflect badly if it comes out that Vinny had been involved in something seedy."

"You've certainly collected a lot of information." PC Grainger seemed to be taking her more seriously now, but she had the impression he still wasn't convinced. "People obviously like to talk to you."

The cryptic statement had her shaking her head. "How do you mean?"

"I mean people keep telling you stuff. I don't know about you, but if I'd killed someone, I'd be keeping very quiet about it, not offloading on random people."

"I think people need to get things off their chest," she said, slowly. "They talk without even really thinking about it."

He nodded. "Can I ask you a question?"

"Yes. Anything."

"Why are you so obsessed with this?" The hint of sympathy in his features, coupled with the same question she kept asking herself, had her squirming.

"I just...I... I..." She searched for a reason which wouldn't make her sound mentally unstable. "I can't shake the feeling that something is amiss. My gut is telling me that Vinny's death wasn't an accident. There was foul play involved."

"You keep telling me how unpleasant he was, so I can't figure out why you even care."

She scrunched her nose up. "Just because he wasn't a good guy, doesn't mean that someone should get away with murder..." Although, as she said it, she was struck by an image of Katie. What if she'd tussled with him and killed him by accident? Would Lily really be okay with seeing her in prison because of it? Or if Oscar had flown into a rage because he wanted to protect his friend.

"I think we need to know the truth," she ventured. "After that it would be up to the courts to decide what happens, right?"

His eyes narrowed and his gaze was intense as he stared at her. "I've just thought of something," he said slowly. "The day before Mr Roth's death, you also argued with him."

"What?" She tilted her head, confused.

"You'd been involved in a heated confrontation with the deceased a mere twenty-four hours before his death."

As that encounter came back to her, Lily tried to speak, but only managed a strangled squeak.

"During that confrontation, you twisted Mr Roth's arm behind his back and made him whimper like a tortured puppy."

"I didn't think you'd seen that," she said, grimacing.

"I turned a blind eye because I figured the guy probably deserved it."

"Okay." She shifted in her seat again. "Surely you're not accusing me of anything?"

"No." Wearily, he shook his head. "But you also don't have an alibi for the time of his death. So I'm pointing out that if you want me to go into detective mode, you'd also be on my list of people to question further." Again, he eyed her intently. "Where did you learn to defend yourself like that, anyway?"

She gave a dismissive shrug, not wanting to get side-tracked. "I did self-defence classes and martial arts when I was younger. I guess it stuck."

Her mind wandered and she pictured her uncle lecturing her on the importance of physical fitness, and how important it was to know how to defend herself. He'd been obsessive about it, which hadn't occurred to Lily as strange until she was older and realised not all little girls were instructed quite so thoroughly on how to kick grown men in the balls with enough force to immobilise them while she ran away. That and a lot of other effective defensive manoeuvres.

"Are you going to look into things more, or not?" Lily demanded, getting the conversation back on track.

PC Grainger's lips twisted to one side. "The problem is there's no concrete evidence of anything. Plus, I'll be honest, it all seems quite far-fetched."

"Does it? Vinny exploited women and was aggressive

towards just about everyone he encountered. Is it really so shocking that someone hit back?"

PC Grainger stretched his neck and looked thoughtful. Presumably, he was searching for the most tactful way to remove Lily from the station.

"You're not going to do anything about it, are you?" she asked with a sinking feeling.

Silently, he shook his head.

It didn't matter, though. She'd told him everything she knew, and that was what she'd intended to do. She rose from the chair. At least she could leave with a sliver of dignity.

"Thank you for listening," she said curtly, and was almost at the door when she gave up on the idea of a dignified exit. "If I could make one quick suggestion," she said with a grimace.

He smiled with warm amusement. "Go on, then."

"I'm absolutely not telling you how to do your job, so please don't take it that way, but I think if I were you I would take a quick look through his things..." She trailed off as PC Grainger's features visibly tensed. Maybe she'd gone too far, but it felt too late to backtrack. "I don't see how it would hurt. If Vinny was up to something dodgy, you could probably find evidence on his laptop."

She was talking quickly again, and was aware that it made her sound like some sort of paranoid, crazy person. The awareness didn't help her slow down. "There's probably a password, so I don't know if you can somehow get around that, but you could at least look. Maybe it's not password protected." She paused and winced at the way PC Grainger was staring at her. "Sorry," she said. "It was just a thought. Although maybe you're not allowed to snoop through his things to look for evidence. Would that make it inadmissible or something?"

He snorted a laugh at that. "You've gone all CSI again," he said lightly.

"About it being inadmissible, or the general idea of searching his things for evidence?"

He squeezed the bridge of his nose. "Looking through his stuff would be my next step too."

"So you will?"

"I already have."

"Oh." So he hadn't entirely dismissed her previous concerns. "Did you get into his laptop?"

"No." His eyes locked with hers in a way that made her self-conscious.

"Was it password protected? I imagine if you're up to something dodgy, there's no way you wouldn't have a password."

"You'd think so," he said wistfully.

Lily searched his features. "You're being cryptic. Was there a password, or not?"

He sighed heavily. "I really shouldn't tell you this." His words had a faraway quality, as though maybe he was thinking aloud. "I will absolutely regret telling you this..."

"Tell me what?" she demanded.

He scratched at his neck and looked annoyed with himself as he spoke his next words. "His laptop seems to have gone missing."

Lily's eyes widened as she hurried back across the room and dropped into the chair.

She had questions for PC Grainger. Lots of them.

Chapter Thirty-Three

FLYNN HAD KNOWN what would happen if he told Lily about the missing laptop. He'd known she'd make a fuss and ask questions he didn't have the answers to. That she'd pin him with her judgemental stare and insist he investigate further.

Maybe that's why he'd told her. Because he wanted someone to lecture him and rant about how he wasn't doing his job properly. After hearing everything Lily had to say, he felt even more certain that he should do more. He should ask questions and look into the situation properly. There'd been a time when he'd have stuck to his convictions and worried about the sergeant later.

Then again, he'd never had a superior so unwilling to listen. And he'd never been in a position where doing the right thing would put his job at risk.

Ten minutes after Lily left the station, he was staring into space, trying to figure out his next move. He could follow her example and dig a little deeper. Ask questions and see where the answers led.

The phone on his desk rang, and he was grateful for the distraction.

"Scilly police station." He answered the phone with his usual greeting.

"You've been trying to call me," the female voice said. "I don't answer the phone when there's no caller ID, and in your message you said you were a police constable, so there was really no way I was going to call you back."

"Sorry," Flynn said. "Can I take your name?"

"Rachel Roth," she replied. "I guess you were calling to tell me that my brother's dead, but I know that now because I read it on social media."

Grimacing, Flynn leaned on the desk. "I'm very sorry you found out that way," he began, softening his tone. "And I'm very sorry for your loss. I know this must be an excruciating time for you, and if I can help in any way, I will."

"Thanks. I do have some questions."

"Of course. If you'd like, I can talk you through what happened to your brother?"

"He slipped and fell off a cliff, right?"

"Yes, that appears to be the case. He was found on a patch of rocks by the sea. There were higher rocks around him that we assume he fell from." He thought about Lily's suspicions and wondered if she was right that it wasn't merely an accident. "It had been raining, so the rocks were slippery..." He took a deep breath, unsure of his next move. Should he suggest it might not have been an accident? If the next of kin requested further investigation, that would scupper Sergeant Proctor's resistance. "As I said, we assume he fell while he was out for a walk, but there would be the option of a post-mortem and further investigation if you requested it."

"I don't care about that," she said.

"Of course." He berated himself for being insensitive. "I'm sorry."

"Don't be sorry," she said, her voice clipped. "I just don't care. I wasn't surprised to hear he's dead. I'm only surprised he lasted this long. Though they say only the good die young, so at that rate he should have lived to a ripe old age."

Flynn's eyes widened, and he opened and closed his mouth a few times without finding any words.

"What I want to know," she said, "is what happens to his stuff? Our parents are both dead, so that makes me his next of kin, doesn't it?"

Shocked at the turn of the conversation, Flynn took a moment to respond. "Yes," he said.

"He borrowed five hundred quid from me. Years ago, it was. But he never paid it back. He laughed at me whenever I asked for it, but I know he's just bought a fancy flat and a new car. Raking it in, he was. So I want to know how I get my money back. And if I get all his stuff and all his money. I'm trying not to get my hopes up, but I'm thinking that having him as a brother might finally pay off."

"I take it you and your brother weren't close?" The question felt redundant, but he asked it anyway.

A burst of laughter hit his ears, then faded quickly. "If I'm his next of kin, that doesn't matter, does it? I can still get his money even if we didn't get on?" She sounded genuinely concerned for the first time in the conversation.

"I'm afraid I can't advise you about inheritance details."

"Can you just tell me if I'll be the one who inherits?"

He frowned. "If you are the next of kin, and he doesn't have a will stating otherwise, then it seems likely that you would inherit."

"Bloody hell, what if he's written a will saying I can't have it? Surely I can still get the money he owes me?"

"I really couldn't say."

"Well, how do I find out? Who do I have to talk to?"

After advising her of her best course of action, Flynn ended the call feeling even more conflicted. On the one hand, he felt more and more certain that further investigation was warranted. On the other hand, the safer course of action for his career would be to keep his head down and not make waves.

He was still mulling over his options when Sergeant Proctor staggered in half an hour later. His pale skin and the fact that it looked as though it was an effort for him to hold himself upright gave the impression he really shouldn't be back at work. But he also wasn't in uniform, so Flynn assumed he wouldn't be staying for long.

"How's everything here?" he asked, heaving in wheezing breaths once he'd dropped into a chair.

"Fine," Flynn replied. "How are you feeling?"

"Rough. I've got a chest infection, but the doctor just prescribed a course of antibiotics, so I expect that'll clear things up quickly."

"Good."

"It looks as though the weather will clear tomorrow, but transport will be chaos with a backlog of visitors trying to get on and off the island. We'll hold off on transporting the body until the following day to avoid adding to the chaos."

"Makes sense," Flynn said. "I spoke to the deceased's sister earlier."

"How did that go?" Sergeant Proctor fished in his pocket for a tissue and blew his bright red nose.

"Fine. She was mostly interested in what she might inherit."

"One of those types, eh?" He made a face as though he were trying to raise an eyebrow but found it too much effort. "You really never know how family members will react."

"She seemed to think her brother had a lot of money," Flynn ventured, knowing he had to tread carefully while he tried once again to convince the sergeant that something shady was going on. "I thought it was odd that a freelance photographer would be so flush."

Sergeant Proctor wiped a hand across his brow. "Don't tell me she got your investigative instincts into gear again? Just because someone has money doesn't make their death suspicious."

"I realise that, but you have to admit that the missing laptop raises questions. I also had Lily Larkin in here again today."

"The woman who found the body?"

"Yes. She's noticed some things that don't add up... and some suspicious behaviour."

Shaking his head, Sergeant Proctor stood. "I thought we were clear about how things stood yesterday."

"Yes." He swallowed hard. "But—"

"Stop it." Sergeant Proctor rounded on him. "You need to understand that small town policing is very different to city policing. Things work differently. You need to drop this idea of starting some investigation which will lead to nothing. A man tragically died, and we dealt with the situation. That's the end of it."

Flynn tried to argue, but was cut off before he could even get a word out.

"I'm not sure you fully appreciate just how thin the ice is that you're teetering on. The only reason I agreed to have you in my station was as a favour to an old colleague. But at this point, I'm not sure there are many people who would be upset about me lodging an official complaint against you. I reckon even your father would be happy if you were forced into a career change." He paused at the door. "Just keep your head down and don't cause trouble. I don't see how that's so difficult."

"It's not," Flynn said, his voice firm and stable despite coming through gritted teeth.

"Good." Sergeant Proctor gave a subtle nod. "I'm off home, but with any luck, I'll be back in the next day or two. Try not to cause any problems between now and then."

Flynn remained rigid in his chair, grateful for the clarity that hit him. He might not like the way Sergeant Proctor did things, but he was his superior and had far more experience than Flynn.

Also, if he wanted to keep his job, it seemed he didn't have much choice but to put the irregularities of the Vincent Roth case out of his head.

Chapter Thirty-Four

THE MISSING LAPTOP really threw Lily's brain into chaos as she walked back to the B&B. It couldn't be a coincidence. Someone was trying to cover up Vinny's illegal activity. She had no doubt about that. PC Grainger had promised to speak to his boss about looking into things further, and she didn't see how they could ignore the mounting evidence. Surely they had plenty of information to launch a proper investigation, and she had the impression PC Grainger was keen to get on with it.

He said he'd call her later and update her. Until then, she planned to do more digging into the owner of the ice cream shop.

Back at the B&B, she was rooting in her pockets for the front door key when the door swung open. Oscar stood before her, wearing the guilt-ridden look of a kid who'd been caught swiping an extra biscuit.

"Hi," Lily said, not moving to the side. "How are you?"

"Fine." He glanced behind him as Flora called his name.

"What's the rush?" she said with an outstretched hand. Discreetly, she pressed a few bank notes into Oscar's palm. "A little holiday bonus. You enjoy your trip."

"We'll see him on the ferry tomorrow," Mr Miller called from behind his wife.

"Oh, yes. We probably will." She looked lighter than the other times Lily had seen her – more relaxed. She said a quick hello to Lily before dashing away with a comment about finishing her packing.

"Are you going away?" Lily asked Oscar when they were alone.

"Just for a little while. Katie's wanted to get away and I said I'd go with her. We're going to rent a car and tour around Cornwall. Stay at campsites."

"Sounds nice," Lily remarked. "Is Katie okay?"

He lifted one shoulder in a shrug. "She's freaking out about everything, but I think a change of scene will help. I hope so, anyway." He smiled sadly. "I hope you enjoy the rest of your holiday."

"Thank you." While Lily watched him leave, her mind slipped back into overdrive.

Katie had been through a lot in the last few weeks, so it was natural that she wanted to get away.

That's what Lily told herself as she ascended the stairs and walked into her room. There was probably no other reason for her sudden desire to leave the island. She was a victim of Vinny's despicable behaviour, nothing more.

Lily was leaving the detective work to the police now, so she didn't need to consider the possibility that Katie was trying to outrun her guilt over killing a guy.

A wave of exhaustion hit her as she sat on the bed with her laptop on her knees. What was she doing? Why couldn't she shut her brain off and relax?

With zero enthusiasm, she typed 'Gail Greenway' into the search bar, then narrowed the search to include 'Isles of Scilly' and 'ice cream shop' when faced with too many results.

She was closer than she'd ever been to solving the mystery

of the photo she'd found in her uncle's possessions, and had never felt less enthusiasm about the subject.

An old article talked about the opening of the ice cream shop, highlighting the fact that the ice cream was homemade on the premises. There was even a photo of the ice cream machines being unloaded from the ship.

A smaller photo showed Gail smiling into the camera. Lily squinted at it but the image wasn't exactly crisp. She thought maybe she recognised the features of the cheery-looking woman, but perhaps it was only that she wanted to recognise her.

Another article reported on the fire at the ice cream shop, including a photo of flames lapping out of the front window of the shop. Quotes from residents expressed sympathy and support for the owner, along with promises to help renovate the shop.

The warmth expressed towards the owner reminded Lily of Mr Greaves' remark that she could be imagining a connection because of the friendliness of the owner.

Since she couldn't find anything current about the owner, it felt like a dead end.

Which was perhaps exactly what Lily needed. As long as there was a lead to follow, she wouldn't be able to help herself, but without an obvious next step she might finally be able to put it behind her.

Besides, she was beginning to feel she'd been moving in the wrong direction all along.

She'd been chasing the past when she should have been building a future.

Chapter Thirty-Five

THURSDAY

ONCE AGAIN, Lily skipped Mrs Miller's breakfast. She'd woken with no appetite and felt utterly flat. The temptation to remain in the bed's warmth was hard to resist, but she forced herself up. Movement would make her feel better. Or so she hoped.

With the house filled with the bustle of everyone getting ready to leave, she ventured out for fresh air. Crossing the quiet lane, she looked out over the beach. Bathed in sunshine, the stretch of sand was bright white and the water beyond glimmered gloriously.

Even the stunning view did nothing to stir Lily's mood, or lift the tiredness she felt deep in her bones. Every night she seemed to sleep worse and worse, and she knew that the lack of rest was affecting her ability to think straight. Perhaps that was why she kept getting swept up in her wild goose chases.

On the path that hugged the top of the beach, she made

her way up the steady incline until she reached the clifftop. Cautiously, she made her way towards the edge, stopping before she got too close. Even with a few metres between her and the ledge she felt a queasiness at the thought of falling. It was hard to imagine anyone wanting to get any closer.

Vinny must have done, though. She took another tiny step, imagining him in his last moments.

He'd been here. Right where she was. Another few steps and his life had been snuffed out. Just like that. Her heart beat faster as she took another step and then one more. Her head spun and every instinct told her to retreat as she jutted out her chin, then stretched her spine to peer over the edge.

In her mind's eye, she imagined him taking one last step. Just one misstep and it was all over. He'd have dropped straight down the bare rock face.

Lily's brain even conjured the thud of a body hitting the rocks after the short plummet.

With a quick intake of breath, she stumbled backwards and out of harm's way. But her heart wouldn't settle and her mind was reeling. She let out a curse and the sound of her own voice seemed to startle her into action.

Something didn't make sense.

She wasn't sure, though. She needed to check from a different angle. Her legs had already burst into a jog.

A couple of minutes later, she was back on the beach and running across it to reach the rocks at the base of the cliff. Pausing, she tried her best to approach in the same way she'd done when she'd found his body.

Because she needed to remember exactly where he'd been.

It took her a few minutes of studying the rocks, waiting for her memory to stir. But then she was there, in the exact spot she'd been when PC Grainger had arrived, looking at the exact spot where Vinny's body had lain.

The scene was tranquil now, with no sign of what had happened less than a week ago.

It was all still there in Lily's head, though.

There for her to study and analyse until she was certain she had everything straight.

Chapter Thirty-Six

"Someone definitely killed him," Lily said when she burst into the police station half an hour later.

As usual, PC Grainger was sitting behind his desk, looking utterly bored.

"Good morning," he said, not reacting to her tone or the fact that she was sweating profusely and no doubt looked a complete state after running the entire way across the island.

"Someone killed him." She sucked in a breath. "All the suspects are about to board the ferry." She heaved another lungful of air as she stood in front of him. She wouldn't sit. There was no time for that. "You need to stop the boat," she said, as firmly as she could while still short of breath. "If you don't stop the boat, the killer will get away."

"Do you have some new evidence for me, Miss Larkin?"

"I do." She clutched at her side. "I was on the rocks this morning," she told him, then shook her head when he gestured for her to sit. "I was on the rocks where Vinny supposedly fell, and I realised there's no way he could have fallen."

His eyebrows drew together. "Why?"

"He was too far from the foot of the rocks," she said, still gasping for breath. "If he'd accidentally stepped off the edge, he'd have dropped like a stone, straight to the bottom. But that's not where he ended up. His body was too far away from the cliff. There are only two ways he could have landed where he did – either he took a running jump, or someone pushed him with force." Panting, she doubled over and pushed her fingers into her side.

"Are you okay?" PC Grainger asked.

She nodded. "I ran here. Got a stitch."

"Do you need a glass of water or something?"

"No. I need you to stop the ferry and figure this whole mess out."

He looked pained, but didn't respond.

"Oh, come on," she said, irritated now. "You can't deny this. I'm talking about laws of physics... if there'd been a ledge for him to hit, that could have propelled him away from the rocks, but there's nothing there. He would have fallen straight down. But he didn't, because someone pushed him."

PC Grainger sighed heavily. "And based on this, you want me to waylay the ferry and disrupt hundreds of people's day?"

"In order to catch a killer, yes. I think it's an entirely reasonable course of action. Also, not just based on this. Based on everything else I've told you."

"And when it turns out that there is no killer? That Mr Roth just slipped and fell? What then?"

"Then we'll be able to sleep better at night knowing we investigated properly."

"I'm not sure how well I'll sleep when I'm out of a job and am suddenly homeless," PC Grainger muttered while massaging the back of his neck.

Lily stared at him for a moment. "Excuse me?"

"Nothing. Ignore me."

"Is that the real issue?" Lily said, frowning as she slipped onto the chair. "You're scared of your boss? Did the sergeant tell you to leave things alone and you don't dare to follow your own instincts?"

"That's how it works in my job," he said wearily. "There's a hierarchy. A chain of command."

"And you won't break that even when you know the sergeant is wrong?"

"I don't *know* that he's wrong."

"Okay," she huffed. "But if it was entirely your decision and there were no consequences, what would you do?"

"There are always consequences," he said, a glimmer of annoyance in his eyes. "And there's a reason more experienced officers get to make the call."

"You'd investigate it though, wouldn't you? Because you agree that I'm onto something, and that something here doesn't add up. Lots of things, actually."

"I'm sorry," he said, looking her right in the eyes. "I can't do anything. My hands are tied."

She resisted the urge to stamp her foot, or throw things, or shout at him. Instead, she held his gaze as though she might will him to grow a backbone.

"What's the worst that can happen?" she said, deciding that getting angry probably wasn't the most effective approach. "If we end up being wrong, you'll get a slap on the wrist, right? Surely you won't get into proper trouble over it."

Finally, he looked away. "In normal circumstances, that would be true," he said. "But..." He sighed and shook his head. "Never mind."

"What?" she prompted.

"I didn't choose to work on the Isles of Scilly," he said slowly, as though nervous he was saying too much. "I'm here as a punishment. The sergeant would love an excuse to make a formal complaint against me. This really isn't the time for me to go rogue."

Realising she was fighting a losing battle, Lily stood. The sense of defeat was almost overwhelming. How could she come so close to figuring things out, only to be thwarted at the last moment?

In the doorway, it came to her that there was one last tactic she could use to try to sway PC Grainger.

He might not help her because it was the right thing to do, or because he believed she was right, but maybe she had one more way to get to him.

She swallowed the lump in her throat.

"Please," she said, the word seeming to hang in the air before her lips.

Briefly, he seemed to consider her plea.

He rubbed his hands down his face before he looked at her. "I'm sorry," he said in a tone that signalled the conversation was over.

PC Grainger's resolve crumbled about three seconds after Lily walked out of the door. The battle he fought with his conscience felt like barely a battle at all. Because he was certain Lily was right. There was more to this case. He wasn't entirely convinced it involved murder, but there was more investigating to be done. That much he knew for sure.

At what cost, though?

Most likely, he'd be looking for a new career.

With a sigh, he pushed back from the desk and crossed the room, contemplating how much he loved his job. Or had done until recently. What he'd been doing in the past month certainly wasn't the job he'd signed up for. Pushing pencils and gaslighting a woman into thinking she was imagining suspicious activity wasn't exactly fulfilling.

But, if he could keep his head down for five more months, he could get back to doing the job he loved in a place he thrived.

Wandering outside and into the road, he caught sight of Lily walking in the opposite direction to the bed and breakfast.

She could be heading down to the harbour to wave off the

ferry, or to a cafe for a morning coffee, but he knew she wasn't. The sureness of her gait told him she was going to do something stupid.

Brave, but stupid.

Squeezing his eyes shut, he let out a low growl. He wanted to be like her – to follow his gut and fight for what he knew was right.

He could still put things right.

It just meant jeopardising his career.

Chapter Thirty-Seven

THE SCILLONIAN LOOMED beside the harbour wall. Lily hadn't yet hatched a plan, but as she hurried towards the ferry, she knew she needed to do something. If PC Grainger wouldn't listen to her, she'd have to get someone else to listen. Shouting accusations loudly might not be a graceful way of going about things, but at least it might get someone's attention. That might force an investigation.

Or she could try to get the attention of the press and cause a stir in the media.

How would she do that, though? She squinted in the bright sunlight, recalling what PC Grainger had said about the locals lodging their grievances via social media. That seemed like a straightforward option.

She was standing beside the ferry, phone in hand, when the broad man at the end of the gangway called out for remaining passengers.

Inwardly, Lily growled. She didn't have time for social media posts. Somehow she needed to stop the ferry, then make herself heard. Requesting to speak to the captain seemed like the logical next move.

Except Lily didn't have a great track record for getting

authority figures to listen to her. She'd had lots of time to convince PC Grainger, to no avail. What if the captain was equally dismissive?

When a young couple approached the guy checking tickets at the end of the gangway, she moved closer, waiting for the guy to turn just a little further.

With a quick hop, she was on the walkway which straddled the water. Another few strides put her on the deck.

"Hey!" the guy called. "I need to see your ticket."

Not looking back, Lily rushed along the deck, ignoring the shouts of the ticket guy.

At the first door she reached, she slipped inside, paying no attention to the passengers sitting on plastic chairs. Sticking to the wall like the amateur spy she apparently was, she moved swiftly. The only attempt to stop her was made by the red fire alarm jutting out of the wall, which made her yelp when she collided with it. Rubbing at the spot on her upper arm, she continued on until she spotted the ladies' toilets and darted inside.

Only then did she fully inflate her lungs. Her heart was thundering and she stared at herself in the mirror, fighting the urge to reflect on what on earth she was doing. She needed to focus on coming up with a plan.

After a couple of minutes of panic, the throbbing in her shoulder gave her the answer she was looking for.

Smothering the rational part of her brain, she retraced her steps, keeping her eyes down until she reached the fire alarm. The bright red paint had a couple of chips in it if you looked closely – possibly from people walking into it. How many other people had it inflicted bruises upon? Maybe not so many, since most people didn't walk with their body pressed to the wall.

Slowly, her hand came up to the lever instructing her to pull in an emergency. That was all it would take. One little tug and the ferry would be forced to delay its departure, buying Lily time to figure out her next move.

With a deep breath, her fingers curled around the lever.

She closed her eyes.

Warmth hit the back of her fingers and her eyelids snapped open to see a hand covering hers.

"Don't," PC Grainger said softly, stepping closer so the scent of him filled her nostrils.

"I have to do something," she said, focusing on keeping the tears that threatened at bay. Her hand remained engulfed by his as her eyes slid up to him.

She lifted a questioning eyebrow. "Did they really call the police because I didn't have a ticket?" She gave a speedy shake of the head. "How did you get here so fast?" Glancing around, she saw the ticket man chatting to another man before they set off at a brisk pace in the other direction. He didn't seem concerned about calling the police on her.

"No one called me," PC Grainger said.

She stared up at him. "Why are you here, then?"

"Because you asked me to help you." The corners of his lips twitched to a reluctant smile that made Lily feel as though her core temperature had increased.

"If I move my hand, will you promise not to set off the fire alarm?" he asked, while his eyes twinkled with affection.

"Maybe."

He lifted an eyebrow. "*Maybe?*"

"What happens next?" she asked.

His hand felt suddenly scorching against hers, but neither of them moved.

"I called the captain on the way here," he said. "He agreed to delay the departure for half an hour, and—" The captain's voice interrupted them, booming over the speaker system to announce the late departure and asking for six passengers to report to the Purser's office by the embarkation hall. As he reeled off the list of names and then repeated them, Lily felt her lips widen to a smile that she felt throughout her body.

"Thank you," she said to PC Grainger.

"No matter what happens next, there's a good chance I'll lose my job." He removed his hand with a stern look that had Lily retreating from the fire alarm. "I only hope that I can at least catch a killer as my last task in the police force." He set off across the room and Lily kept pace with him. "You'd better be right about this."

"I'm almost certain I'm right," she said.

"*Almost* certain'" He stopped at the foot of the stairs and looked at her sharply. "You sounded much more confident at the station earlier."

"I'm like 97 percent sure." She winced. "Or maybe 95... There's a very good chance, anyway."

"Bloody hell," he muttered. "We should hurry before the odds dive even further."

His long legs took the stairs two at a time with ease, while Lily's legs worked double time to keep up.

"What's the plan?" he asked when they reached the embarkation hall and he stopped a few metres from an open door which Mr and Mrs Miller had just walked through.

"The plan?" Her insides had turned to mush and her smile was just as watery. The more she thought about it, the less sure she was in her convictions. Her knees felt as though they might buckle and it occurred to her that might not be a bad thing. Could she pass out and wake up in a completely different reality? One where she wasn't about to make a fool of herself and get a perfectly good police officer sacked.

Maybe he wasn't perfectly good, though. He was probably incompetent and she was doing society a favour by forcing a career change on him. That's what she'd tell herself if he lost his job.

"Lily," he said, the gravity of his voice grounding her.

"Yeah?"

"What was your plan? Once you'd pulled the fire alarm?"

She winced. "I hadn't got that far. I guess I was probably going to accuse people of murder and see what happened. But if you have a different plan – any other plan at all – I think we should go with yours."

His gaze drifted over her shoulder, lingering somewhere in the middle distance. "It's not actually a terrible plan."

"Accusing people of murder?" She laughed. "It's a really terrible plan."

He shook his head. "Sometimes, in policing, we bluff... Pretend we know more than we do and see how people react."

"So you want to pretend you know that one of them killed Vinny and ask the murderer to step forward?"

"No." He smiled. "I don't want to accuse *all* of them. I want to put pressure on the person who killed Vinny and see if they crack."

"Small problem," she pointed out. "We don't know who did it."

"Just give me your best guess..."

"I can't," she said wildly. "I don't know."

"Okay." He walked forward and put a hand on the door. "I'll give you about three minutes to figure it out."

Chapter Thirty-Eight

FROM LILY'S point of view, PC Grainger seemed to grow about a foot as he stepped into the windowless room with a large desk at one side and a small table with a few plastic chairs at the other.

"Sorry to disrupt your schedule," he said to the captain in a tone that commanded the attention of everyone in the room. "Hopefully, I won't keep you long."

"Happy to help," the captain said, while looking utterly torn, as though he wanted to be annoyed but was responding instinctively to PC Grainger's manner. "Should I...?" He indicated the door.

"You can stay," PC Grainger said, before briefly scrutinising each of the other people in the room.

"Is there a problem?" Alanna asked haughtily. "Because we've been wanting to get away from these islands for days and I'd appreciate you not messing things up now that the weather is cooperating."

"I've no desire to hold anyone up," PC Grainger said. "Unfortunately, we do have a problem, though." A frown wrinkled his forehead, giving him an even sterner demeanour. "As you may guess, it's concerning the death of Mr Vincent

Roth. Sadly, what initially appeared to be a tragic accident may not have been that at all." He paused, seemingly observing the reactions in the room.

Lily did the same, noticing the quiet gasp from Mrs Miller and the way Alanna bit down on her lip as she wrung her hands.

"What on earth are you suggesting?" Mr Miller asked.

"I don't like to suggest anything," PC Grainger replied. "I'm informing you that we're launching an investigation into Mr Roth's death. We're no longer satisfied it was an accident."

"You think someone killed him?" Mr Miller asked.

"Oh, my god," Alanna whispered, clutching at Marc's arm.

"Murder?" Flora's voice came out high-pitched. "You can't be serious?"

Deadly, Lily thought and stifled a laugh at her inappropriate sense of humour. Then she kept her gaze firmly on PC Grainger since focusing on his fierce demeanour seemed the best way to ward off an extremely inappropriate fit of the giggles.

"We've already been gathering evidence," PC Grainger informed those in front of him. "Once the forensic team is involved, it shouldn't take long to build a clear picture of the exact nature of Mr Roth's death."

"Why did you stop the boat?" Oscar asked, a protective arm around Katie, who'd lost all the colour from her cheeks.

"Given that you were all in contact with the deceased in the days leading up to his death, we will need to interview you all more thoroughly."

"So we're stuck here?" Alanna asked. "You're saying we're not allowed to leave?"

"I don't think he's saying that." Marc slipped an arm around Alanna's waist while his eyes went to PC Grainger. "Are you?"

"I won't be forcing anyone to stay," PC Grainger replied levelly. "But given the gravity of the situation, I'm asking you all to stay on the island voluntarily while we carry out our investigation."

Good move, Lily thought. As inconvenient as it was, anyone who was innocent shouldn't put up too much of a fuss about staying.

"I just want to see my daughter," Mrs Miller said through a sob. "And my grandchildren. Is that too much to ask?"

"You can," Rodney told her. "He said it was voluntary. That means we can still go if we want."

"You are absolutely at liberty to leave if you choose," PC Grainger said, still sounding utterly calm and in control. "However, we would be extremely grateful for your cooperation with our investigation. And, as I mentioned, once the forensic team is involved, we expect to get answers quickly. If any of you have failed to mention anything which would contribute to the investigation, it would be in your own interests to amend that now."

"Oh, my goodness!" Mrs Miller covered her face with her hands momentarily. Then removed them to glare at her husband. "You have to tell him everything."

Rodney stared back at her.

"Just tell him the truth and we'll figure it out together."

"The truth?" Mr Miller said, doing a fantastic impression of a man who had no clue what his wife was talking about.

"About where you were when Vinny died," Mrs Miller said. "You lied to the police. But all lies come out, eventually."

Chapter Thirty-Nine

IT ALL FELT a bit too easy.

That was Lily's thought as she watched Mr and Mrs Miller stare at each other contemptuously. She was supposed to give PC Grainger an indication of who he should put pressure on, but apparently that might not even be necessary. Maybe Mrs Miller was about to incriminate her own husband.

"What the heck are you talking about?" Mr Miller asked with a pinched expression.

Mrs Miller propped her hands on her hips. "You told the officer you were with me when Vinny died, but you weren't. I can't see why you'd lie about that... unless." She swallowed hard. "If the two of you got into an argument and something happened... an accident... you just need to explain it. Everything will be all right in the end."

Rodney's eyes showed no emotion whatsoever. His face was a picture of confusion. "I was with you when he died," he said slowly. "I saw Vinny leave the house and then I came into the kitchen..."

"But then you left again!" Flora's voice rose in both volume and pitch. "You said you helped me with breakfast, but you didn't. Not straightaway. You came in and then you left for a while before coming back to help."

"To have a shower," he said, speaking to her as though she were stupid. "I had a shower and then I came back into the kitchen. I must have been away from you for ten minutes at the most."

"Exactly," she said. "How can you say you were with me when you were in the shower? It's not as though I watched you shower."

It took Rodney a moment to react, but when he did, it was with a burst of laughter. "Good god! Do you honestly think I killed the fella?" This time his laughter had a manic note to it. "You think I've killed some poor fella because he complained about your burnt bacon?"

"So you didn't do it?" Mrs Miller asked sheepishly.

"Thirty years of marriage and you think I'm capable of killing a man? That's a little disturbing, love." He shook his head at his wife, who seemed to shrink into herself.

"I just don't understand why you didn't tell the police to start with that you were in the shower," Flora whispered.

"Maybe because I didn't realise I was on trial for murder! I said I was at home, with you. Which I was. I didn't know I had to account for every minute of that." He turned to PC Grainger. "I was in the shower and away from my wife's sight for about five minutes at the time of Mr Roth's death." He folded his arms across his chest. "From now on, I reckon I might spend a lot more time out of my wife's sight."

"Don't be like that," Flora said, reaching for her husband, only to be shrugged off. "A man had died, and I was panicking. And now PC Grainger is saying it wasn't an accident, so I was right to have panicked."

"What makes you think it wasn't an accident?" Mr Miller asked, rolling his eyes.

PC Grainger's gaze slid momentarily to Lily, silently reminding her of the plan. He needed to know who killed

Vinny, and she still couldn't figure it out. Mr and Mrs Miller seemed highly unlikely now, which left Katie or Oscar, or Alanna or Marc. She hoped it wasn't Katie or Oscar, but they both looked shifty enough that she couldn't rule them out. Alanna also didn't exactly look the picture of innocence as she sniffed loudly every few seconds and kept muttering about the stress of it all. Beside her, Marc was his usual calm and collected self.

Lily's gaze went to PC Grainger as he started talking again, but her eyes quickly bounced back to Marc. PC Grainger's words resounded loudly in her head. Not the ones he was currently saying – about the positioning of the body and the trajectory of the fall – but ones he'd spoken days before.

If I'd killed someone, I'd be keeping very quiet.

He was right. Anyone with something to hide would be careful what they said. Almost everyone in the room had happily confided in Lily and made no effort to conceal their emotions.

Marc, on the other hand, had kept quietly in the background, not drawing the slightest bit of attention to himself.

On a physical level, he was surely the one most likely to overpower Vinny. He could also have slipped away with no one noticing. From what Lily had observed, he tended to go downstairs for a coffee before Alanna in the mornings.

He also had access to the memory card and the laptop.

He probably knew what Vinny had been up to, and decided to put a stop to it.

Lily needed time to ponder it more. Except she didn't have time.

Her eyes swept over everyone in the room as PC Grainger continued to speak in his levelled voice. He was doing brilliantly, but he'd run out of steam soon and would need Lily's input.

He didn't need to know for definite, she told herself. He'd

only asked for her best guess. Right now, her best guess was Marc. As discreetly as she could manage, she pulled her phone from her pocket and opened a blank document. With a slight tremble to her fingers, she typed out two words.

Marc.

Laptop?

Then she inched closer to PC Grainger and kept her eyes on her phone as though reading a message. With the slightest movement, she nudged PC Grainger's arm with her elbow, then angled the phone a few degrees in his direction.

He didn't pause in his monologue, and she couldn't even be sure he'd read it until he changed the direction of his little speech.

"We also have the issue of some missing items. While Mr Roth's camera was recovered, it appears a memory card has gone missing, along with his laptop. I'm sure none of you will object to a search. I'll start here with your hand luggage and check any other luggage later."

Lily caught the way Marc's fingers wrapped more tightly around the strap of his backpack.

"If I could start with you?" PC Grainger's gaze landed firmly on Marc.

The bob of his Adam's apple was his only sign of distress. "Don't you need a warrant for that?" he asked, with a small smile. "I'm sure no one wants the contents of their bags being strewn around in front of everyone."

"I promise not to strew anything around," PC Grainger said, taking a step forwards and extending his hand for the bag. "I'll just take a quick look inside."

"Surely you need a warrant, though," Marc said, keeping a firm grip on his bag.

"No," PC Grainger said. "I don't. I'm permitted to conduct a search if I feel there's enough suspicion. But I also imagine you'll all be willing to cooperate to help with the investigation."

With a shake of her head, Alanna turned on Marc. "Just show him what's in your bag and then we can leave." She pulled on the zip of her oversized handbag and opened it in PC Grainger's direction. "Let's all just show him," she went on. "He's only doing his job. Then we can all get on our way."

As everyone else opened their bags, Marc kept a hold of his.

"May I?" PC Grainger said, his hand still outstretched.

"Oh, my goodness." Alanna snatched it from Marc and handed it over. "What on earth is the problem? He only wants a quick look."

Lily let out a silent sigh of relief.

Unless she was very much mistaken, her best guess was spot on.

Chapter Forty

"It's not how it looks," Marc said, when PC Grainger pulled two laptops from his bag.

"Really?" PC Grainger asked while drawing a zipper bag containing memory cards from the backpack. "I'm going to need you to explain all of this then, so I don't jump to the wrong conclusion."

While everyone else seemed to take a step back, Alanna shot to Marc's side, eyes darting between his face and the laptops. "Why have you got Vinny's computer?" she asked. "And what are these?" She pointed at the bag of memory cards.

"Look..." Marc exhaled a frustrated sigh. "I really didn't want you to know about this."

"About what?" she spat.

"Vinny was into some dodgy stuff."

"What kind of dodgy stuff?"

Marc shook his head, but still didn't look overly concerned by the situation. "He took photos of women and he had a website where people could view them."

"Right," Alanna said. "What's so bad about that?"

"Pornography," Lily supplied gently. "Sometimes the

women were terrified teenagers." She stopped talking when PC Grainger's eyes landed on her. "I think," she mumbled and shrank back out of the conversation.

Alanna blinked rapidly. "No. That can't be right." Her eyes widened when realisation dawned on her. "The women who kept posting nasty comments on my blog?"

Marc nodded. "That's another reason I told him to stop. It was hurting your business and I couldn't have that."

"Could I ask why you tried to cover this up after Mr Roth's death?" PC Grainger asked.

"I thought it would be upsetting for people if it came out. And I didn't really see the need for it to come to light. Vinny's dead, and the website is shut down."

"How was the website shut down?" PC Grainger asked.

"I had his laptop," Marc said, as though it was obvious.

"And you just happened to know his password and all the details of his illegal activity?" PC Grainger pressed.

"I already told you I knew about it."

"You must have known a lot, though, in order to put a stop to it." PC Grainger tilted his chin. "Were you involved in this illegal activity, too?"

"No." He shook his head. "Definitely not."

PC Grainger puffed his chest out. "I should inform you that the investigation will be thorough. That includes going into your phone records and bank records. If you had any involvement, we will find out. If you're lying now, it will make things much worse for you later."

The entire room fell utterly silent.

"I might have been helping him out a bit..."

Alanna gasped and clutched at the back of the chair beside her as though she needed the physical support. "This can't be happening," she muttered and then gasped again. "When did Vinny start all this?" she asked Marc forcefully.

"A couple of years ago."

Tears filled her eyes. "About the time you got a new job?"

she asked angrily. "Your well-paid job in website design and maintenance?" She shook her head in disgust. "How could you?"

"You always wanted me to travel with you? It was you who suggested I get a job where I could work remotely. And somehow you expected me to afford flights to all the fancy destinations you wanted to go to."

Alanna continued to shake her head. "You're sick," she said. "I was telling my female followers to empower themselves and all the time you and Vinny were exploiting women right under my nose. How didn't I see this?"

"It's not your fault," Mrs Miller said kindly, approaching Alanna and giving her shoulder a sympathetic pat.

PC Grainger spoke again, directing his words at Marc. "I'm going to need to ask you again where you were at the time of Mr Roth's death. And I would remind you that our forensic technology is highly sophisticated. We'll be able to build a clear picture from fibres and fabrics on the corpse so it would be much better if you provide us with anything you know about his death."

Marc ran a hand down his face, but still didn't appear overly stressed. "I messaged him that morning, asking him to meet me. I only wanted to talk to him."

"What happened?" PC Grainger asked.

"We talked. I told him we needed to stop all that seedy business before we got into real trouble."

"What did he say?" Alanna whispered.

"He wouldn't listen to reason. He'd got greedy and wanted more and more money. He wasn't going to stop."

Alanna's hands came up to her ashen face. "What did you do?"

"It was self-defence really," Marc said in a rush. "He pushed me, so I pushed him back."

"Oh my god," Alanna muttered, taking steps back. "You killed him. You actually killed him."

When Marc took a step towards Alanna, PC Grainger calmly put himself between them.

"You should thank me," Marc said to Alanna. "I did you a favour. You wanted him out of the business."

"Not like this," she said, her voice trembling. "I didn't want him dead."

"I'm going to need you to come back to the station with me," PC Grainger told Marc.

He shrugged. "I'm not saying anything else until I have a lawyer."

"I think that's an excellent idea." PC Grainger removed his handcuffs from his belt. "Do I need these, or will you come without a fuss?"

"I'll come," he said, then looked at Alanna. "We'll get all of this sorted out, babe. Once they realise what kind of person Vinny was, no one's going to be too concerned with what I did. It'll all blow over."

Lily's eyes widened at the look on Marc's face – as though he truly believed what he was saying. He genuinely didn't think he'd done anything wrong.

He actually thought he could get away with killing someone because the victim wasn't a nice guy.

She suspected he was in for quite a shock.

Chapter Forty-One

When PC Grainger led Marc out of the room, the rest of them automatically followed. Lily kept her eyes on PC Grainger's back while they made their way off the ship, so was only vaguely aware of Alanna sobbing about how it would be the end of her career. Mr Miller quietly consoled her with the reasoning that no publicity was bad publicity. She calmed down at that, asking if he thought it might be a positive thing for her blog.

Passengers stood on the deck, watching them file off via the gangway. Back on dry land a small crowd had formed. Apparently the ferry being held up had caused quite the spectacle. The chatter seemed to halt, and all eyes fell to PC Grainger, but he didn't stop, just continued on his way with a hand firmly on Marc's arm. He hadn't gone far when he glanced over his shoulder and met Lily's eye. His lips remained in a hard line, but the way his eyes bored into hers felt distinctly like a secret high-five.

Once he was out of sight, Lily tuned back into the conversations around her.

"I don't know what to do," Alanna was saying manically to Mr and Mrs Miller. "PC Grainger said I was free to leave and he would contact me by phone later about making a statement, but it feels strange to leave now. Like I'm running away or something. I think I want to stay for a little while. Could I stay with you for another day or two?"

"Of course," Mrs Miller said. "We'll take care of you."

"Aren't we getting the ferry, then?" Rodney asked his wife.

"No. We'll stay and look after Alanna. We can't leave her alone after all this."

Alanna murmured her thanks, while Rodney looked bemused.

"I thought you were desperate to get away," he said.

"I was, yes. But that was before..."

"Oh, I see! That was back when you thought you were married to a murderer? Is that why you wanted to go to Kerry's place – so you weren't alone with your monster of a husband?"

"I'm never going to hear the end of this, am I?" Mrs Miller said frostily. "One mistake and it'll haunt me forever."

"Quite a hefty mistake," Rodney said dryly.

"Have some compassion," Flora growled through gritted teeth. "Imagine what I've been going through. On top of everything, I had the guilt of knowing it was all my fault that you'd got so angry with Vinny. If I hadn't burned the bacon, you'd never have argued with him."

Mr Miller looked perplexed by the turn of the conversation. "It's not as though you burned the bacon on purpose." His eyes widened as the truth dawned. "Oh, my goodness. You've been trying to get bad reviews, haven't you?"

"I kept telling you I wanted to be closer to the grandchildren," Flora replied sadly. "You wouldn't listen."

"I feel as though it's me who's been living with a monster," Mr Miller grumbled without a lot of conviction.

Alanna started to cry into a wad of tissues.

"Sorry, love," Mr Miller said sheepishly. "That was insensitive. This must be awful for you."

"We've been together for ten years," she said. "I can't believe all of this."

Mrs Miller rubbed Alanna's back while mumbling sympathetic words.

"If we're not going anywhere, I better see about getting our luggage off the boat," Mr Miller said.

"Get Alanna's things too," his wife instructed him. He left immediately, while Flora continued to comfort Alanna.

"I don't think I want to go anywhere now either," Katie said, from behind Lily. She'd remained tightly by Oscar's side the whole time. Lily turned and watched her look up at him with big, sorrowful eyes. "I'm sorry. I begged you to come with me and now I don't want to go."

"It's fine," Oscar said. "We'll stay here. I'll grab our bags." He looked at Lily, silently telling her to keep an eye on Katie.

Lily moved to stand beside Katie, but she'd got her phone out and was too busy tapping away to notice.

"Are you okay?" Lily asked after a moment.

She sniffed as she looked up from her phone. "I messaged my mum and asked her to come and get me. I'm going to tell her everything."

"That's probably a good idea."

"I suppose I'll need to speak to the police about it, so my parents will find out, anyway."

"Everything will be okay," Lily said gently.

"Yeah." She drew in a deep breath. "My mum will be fine about it. My dad will probably freak out."

"It's probably still better to have it all out in the open."

"I think you're right." She got distracted by Mrs Miller waving her arms around.

"My neighbour, Tina, is over there," she told them. "I'm going to ask if she can drive us home. Do you want to come with us, Lily?"

"No, thank you. I'll catch up with you later."

"Okay." Flora patted her arm. "I'll make you a nice cup of

225

tea when you get back. With lots of sugar. That's what we'll all need after the shock of this morning."

"Thank you," Lily said, while trying not to grimace at the thought of her sugary tea. "I'll see you later."

Mrs Miller waved Mr Miller over as she led Alanna away. Oscar was just stepping off the ferry as well, laden down with bags.

"He's been so sweet," Katie said quietly to Lily. "We were at school together, but I didn't really know him properly until the last few weeks. He's really lovely." Her cheeks pinked and she turned her face away as Oscar walked towards them.

"Got it," he said, depositing Katie's compact suitcase by her feet.

"Thank you," she told him shyly. "I messaged my mum. She said she'd come straightaway and take me home. I'm going to have to explain everything."

Oscar rubbed her upper arm. "It'll be okay. Your mum will understand when you explain it all."

"I think so."

They spent the next five minutes dissecting everything that had happened on the boat and exclaiming over how shocked they were by Marc's confession. Then Katie's mum arrived and bundled her into her car, looking sympathetic and concerned without yet knowing what had happened.

"I really like her," Oscar said, remaining by Lily as they watched the car drive away.

"Katie?"

"Yes."

"I think she really likes you, too."

He shoved his hands into his pockets. "She's going to hate me when she finds out what I did."

As the car turned the corner, Lily turned to look questioningly at Oscar.

"I looked at the photos," he said. "I promised her I wouldn't, but I did. I don't know why I looked at them."

Lily smiled gently. "You had naked photos of the girl you like. It's not really that shocking that you looked at them."

"But I'd promised her I wouldn't."

"I wouldn't beat yourself up over it too much," Lily said.

"I have to tell her, though, don't I?" He looked at her as though she were the fountain of all knowledge. All she could do was shrug. "I definitely have to," he went on. "I can't keep lying to her. If she hates me for it, that's probably what I deserve."

Lily shook her head. "We all make mistakes. Tell her and apologise. If it were me, I'd be furious, but I suspect she might forgive you."

He shifted his weight, eyes fixed on his shoes. "The photos freaked me out. I thought they'd be different, but she looked so scared in them. That's why I left the memory card in the camera bag when I handed it in. I thought people should know that he wasn't a good person. Even if he was dead, I thought people should know."

"He definitely wasn't a nice guy," Lily said.

"What happened to the memory card?" Oscar asked. "I guess Marc took it, but how?"

"After you gave the camera to Mrs Miller, she gave it to Alanna so she could download the photos before it was handed to the police. Marc would have had a chance to get the memory card then."

"That's another thing I need to explain to Katie; that I purposely tried to get the memory card to the police instead of keeping it like she wanted. She still doesn't know that I don't have it. She thinks I've been keeping it hidden all this time." He dragged his hands through his hair, then seemed to gather himself. He picked up his duffel bag and slung it over his shoulder. "Do you want me to walk you back to the Miller's?"

"No, thanks." She wasn't sure what she was going to do, but she didn't want to head back there just yet.

"Are you okay?" Oscar asked, giving her arm a squeeze.

"I think so. Still a bit shocked." She glanced at the ferry, trying to comprehend the morning's events. "You get going though. I might just go for a walk or something."

"You're leaving tomorrow, right?"

"Yeah." She'd forgotten about that. The week seemed to have gone by in a blink, and the thought of leaving made her stomach feel heavy.

"I might not see you again." Oscar looked at her sadly, then surprised her by gathering her into a hug. "Thanks for everything," he said before flashing her a bashful smile and striding away.

"Bye," she muttered, ignoring the way her stomach tightened even further.

Oscar was barely out of her sight when a familiar voice called Lily's name. Seren and Kit were walking hastily towards her.

"Are you okay?" Seren asked, placing a hand on Lily's forearm. "We heard the police ordered the ferry to stop, and that someone was arrested. Something to do with that guy who fell from the cliff."

Lily nodded. "I stopped a killer from getting away," she said, the words sounding strange, but also giving her a distinct tingle of pride. After spending half the week doubting herself, it felt good to find that she hadn't been going completely crazy. She laughed at the shocked expressions of Seren and Kit.

"*You?*" Kit asked. "You stopped a killer?"

"Yeah." She couldn't stop grinning now. "I did. With just a little help from PC Grainger."

Seren's eyebrows rose steadily upwards. "Why do I feel this story needs to be told over drinks?"

Lily checked her watch, having lost all sense of time. It wasn't quite midday, but it also wasn't far off. "I could definitely use a drink," she said. "And food. I haven't eaten anything today."

"Right." Seren linked her arm through Lily's. "We're

getting you food and a drink. And then you can tell us everything."

"It might take a while," Lily said, thinking back on all that had happened over the last week.

"We have time," Seren said, as the three of them set off walking toward the pub.

Chapter Forty-Two

Sergeant Proctor burst into the police station just as Flynn was walking back out from the cells. With Marc locked up, he thought he would finally get a moment to breathe, but judging by the sergeant's strained expression, that probably wasn't going to happen.

"What the hell is going on?" he fumed. "I heard the ferry was delayed. And the rumour is it was delayed because of a police request."

"A rumour?" Flynn asked, certain that Sergeant Proctor wouldn't rely on gossip.

"I heard it from the captain himself," he spat.

"Hardly a rumour then," Flynn pointed out, taking a seat at his desk. Now that he had a criminal in custody, he was less concerned about Sergeant Proctor's reaction to the events of the day. Crimes had been committed and Flynn had acted accordingly. The sergeant might have his feathers ruffled for not being involved, but there was no official reason for him to reprimand Flynn.

"Don't get smart with me," the sergeant snarled. "I told you to leave things be, and you've gone off on some wild quest because you don't understand how small-town policing works.

You just want drama, and I can tell you now that you won't find it here."

Flynn waited patiently for him to finish his rant. "I got a confession," he said casually.

"You got what?" Sergeant Proctor's features scrunched up. "A confession from who? About what?"

"From Marc Collins. He confessed to being involved in the death of Mr Vincent Roth."

The sergeant's eyes bulged, and a muscle in his jaw twitched. "Where is he now?" he finally asked.

"In cell one." Flynn tilted his head in that direction.

"I'm assuming you read him his rights?" The tone of his voice suggested that he actually assumed the opposite. If he genuinely thought him that incompetent, there was no wonder he resented having him around.

"Yes," Flynn said through gritted teeth.

"Bloody hell." Sergeant Proctor started towards the cells.

"There's more," Flynn said, stopping him in his tracks.

"More?" he echoed.

With great effort, Flynn refrained from rolling his eyes at the sergeant's exasperated tone. "It seems the suspect and the deceased were involved in illegal activity together."

"What kind of illegal activity?" the sergeant growled, as though the crimes were Flynn's fault.

"Vincent Roth was coercing young women into naked photoshoots," he stated flatly. "Later he and Marc uploaded the photos to an internet site. In some cases, I believe they blackmailed the women to keep them from reporting it. And it seems that some of the women were underage teenagers."

The sergeant stood rooted to the spot. "You have proof of this?"

"Yes, sarge."

In a rush of movement, he stalked to the window and threw his hands up. "For Christ's sake," he grumbled, then turned and glared at Flynn.

PC Grainger felt nothing but annoyance. "You realise I haven't done anything wrong," he said firmly.

"That's yet to be established." He strode over to the chair opposite Flynn and sat heavily. "You better tell me everything from the beginning. Let's just hope you've done everything by the book."

Obediently, Flynn opened his notepad.

It took the best part of an hour for him to debrief the sergeant, and then another couple of hours to write up his report.

The sergeant, apparently in better health, spent that time making phone calls to their colleagues on the mainland – making a plan for moving Marc over there.

With his report finished, Flynn waited for the sergeant to finish his latest phone call.

"I could escort the prisoner tomorrow," Flynn suggested. Maybe the offer would help get him in the sergeant's good books. It would also mean a day away from the Scillies. Some time back in civilisation would be a welcome relief.

Sergeant Proctor sighed. "I'll think about it."

"I can also sleep at the station tonight if you want me to stay with the prisoner." Someone needed to be there. "If you're still not feeling great..."

"I'm fine," he grumbled. "You can go home. I'll handle things from here."

"If you're sure..." He could have sworn he detected a softening of the sergeant's tone. That could only be a good thing.

"See you tomorrow, PC Grainger," he said without glancing up from the paperwork in front of him.

Chapter Forty-Three

It occurred to Lily that PC Grainger had meant it in an official sense when he'd said he'd call her. Really, he'd probably meant that *someone* would be in touch – not necessarily him, and not necessarily soon. That didn't stop her from checking her phone regularly over the course of the day.

Over lunch in the pub she'd told Seren and Kit – and a few others – about the events of the morning. When Kit had to get to work, he insisted on taking Lily with him.

She felt like a VIP sitting at the front of the electric train with him. His charisma, combined with his extensive knowledge of the islands, turned what she expected to be a cute tour of the island into a riveting hour that went by in a blink. It was a testament to how excellent he was at his job that he could keep Lily's attention so effortlessly given all that was going on in her head.

"That was exactly what I needed today," she said at the end of the tour. "Thank you."

"You're welcome." He hopped out of the train, then turned back to her. "By the way, was my mum useful with her information about the owner of the ice cream shop?"

"She remembered the name of the owner so that was really helpful."

His smile was full of warmth. "So you found what you were looking for?"

"I don't know." She pressed her lips together. "I'm not sure what I was looking for. And I'm not convinced there was anything to be found." But maybe that was exactly the answer she needed so she could start making plans for her future.

A small boy appeared beside Kit's legs, interrupting them. "Can you make me a balloon animal?" he asked. Kit had promised them to anyone who wanted one at the end of the tour.

"What's your favourite animal?" Kit asked.

"A sloth."

Kit smiled lightly. "Do they look anything like giraffes?"

"No," the boy said.

"How about if you squint? I'll bet they look like giraffes then."

The boy stared up at Kit. "I don't think so."

"I'll leave you to it," Lily said, exiting the train and walking around the front of it. "Thanks again for the ride, and for lunch... and everything."

"I should thank you," he said. "For keeping us all safe with your detective work."

"I didn't really do anything."

"Are you kidding? Marc would have got away scot-free if it weren't for you. You were amazing."

"Thank you," she said, despite feeling that he was giving her too much credit.

In a display of affection that she was getting used to, he opened his arms and wrapped her in a hug. Not the perfunctory kind, but a tight embrace that felt as though he was in no rush at all, despite the queue of children that had gathered behind him.

When they broke apart, Lily felt a hollowness in her stomach. She barely knew Kit, so she knew it wasn't really saying goodbye to him that was the issue. It was that she suddenly felt her life was full of goodbyes and she was sick of it. Tomorrow she had to go back to her cold, empty flat and her empty life. The thought filled her with dread.

"If you can't make a sloth," the boy said loudly, "can you make a hermit crab? I really like them too."

Kit grimaced in Lily's direction. "I reckon I can make a sloth after all." He flashed Lily a wink and pulled a long yellow balloon from a container in the train.

Smiling, Lily backed away. Once again, she checked her phone, but there was still nothing from PC Grainger. With nothing else to do, she headed back to the bed and breakfast, feeling suddenly exhausted.

Chapter Forty-Four

FRIDAY

WALKING BACK into work the following day, Flynn felt he was holding his breath to see what mood Sergeant Proctor was in, and whether he really might be thawing towards him.

The sergeant smiled at him, which was definitely progress.

"I was just thinking about you," he said in a tone that gave nothing away. "I reckon you've earned yourself some holiday time."

It was about the last thing Flynn expected to hear. Even though he'd been covering for his colleagues for the past week, he hadn't expected the sergeant to acknowledge that. He had a sudden rush of hope that the next five months might actually pass pleasantly.

"Thanks." A spark of anticipation hit him. If he had time off, he could get back to civilised society for a while. A couple of nights out with his mates would put everything into perspective. "If I escort the prisoner over to the mainland, I could take a few days over there."

"No," Sergeant Proctor mused. "PC Hill is going to take him."

That made no sense. If Flynn had time off and planned to get back home anyway—

"I'll need you on the island." The smile his sergeant offered turned to a smirk. "With PC Hill away, you'll need to be around in case there are any emergencies."

Flynn frowned, knowing how slim the chances of an emergency were. "But—"

"No buts. You enjoy your time off. I'll see you in a week." Casually, he turned and walked in the direction of the cells.

"What am I supposed to do with time off if I can't leave the island?" Flynn called. He realised exactly what the sergeant was up to. Time off wasn't a reward; it was a punishment.

Sergeant Proctor turned back and sneered. "My first suggestion would be to go home and get yourself out of that uniform." He didn't add that he didn't deserve to wear it, but the inference was loud and clear.

Flynn stared after him, trying to think of the best course of action.

It didn't take him long to figure it out: stick to his original plan to keep his mouth shut, his head down and try to get through the next five months while making as few waves as possible.

He left the station with his jaw so tight he was probably damaging his teeth. Stalking quickly back to his flat, he tried not to let his anger get the better of him. The best thing to do would be to take Sergeant Proctor at his word and enjoy a week off. Technically, it was a holiday, even if it felt distinctly like a suspension.

To avoid getting further sucked down by his negative thoughts, he didn't linger in the flat, but left again as soon as he'd changed.

The ferry didn't leave for almost an hour, so he assumed Lily would still be over at the Miller's place.

On instinct, he set off in that direction.

Chapter Forty-Five

On her last morning on the island, Lily packed her things, then had breakfast with a shell-shocked Alanna. It turned out Mrs Miller could make an excellent fry up when she wasn't on a mission to incite negative reviews.

Mr Miller offered to drive Lily to the ferry, but she was happy to walk across the island one last time. She also had a stop or two to make on her way. Her desire to speak to PC Grainger one last time was only natural, she told herself as she walked. It occurred to her it would mean saying another goodbye, and the thought of it brought a heaviness to her chest.

As someone who'd spent most of her childhood moving from one place to another, it felt odd to be suddenly having such a hard time saying goodbye to people. At least until she realised that her upbringing hadn't even given her the opportunity to say farewell whenever they moved to the next place. Suddenly, that didn't seem like a bad strategy.

She could go straight to the ferry and not bother saying goodbye to PC Grainger. That was what she was thinking about at the exact moment that she spotted him walking towards her. Her smile came automatically, and she felt suddenly idiotic for thinking that she might just slip away without seeing him again.

"Good morning, PC Grainger," she said brightly.

"Flynn," he said, grinning. "Good morning to you, too. I was just on my way to find you."

Warmth pooled in her stomach as they stopped in front of each other. In a pair of blue jeans and a black T-shirt, he looked way more casual than the other times she'd seen him.

"Sorry," she said, realising she was staring. "This is the first time I've seen you out of uniform. Up close anyway. It's a little disconcerting."

"For me too." His smile slipped away and Lily had the distinct feeling she'd said the wrong thing.

"Are you okay?" she asked.

"Yeah. I just like my uniform and..." He gave a quick shake of the head and his lips pulled into an unconvincing smile. "The sergeant rewarded my efforts yesterday with some time off."

"You got suspended?" she said, her voice coming out louder than expected.

"No. Not officially. I got a week's holiday. Except I'm not allowed to leave the islands."

Lily frowned, annoyed on his behalf. "I think you should get a promotion. Or a medal maybe."

"A medal?" He laughed at that, then glanced at her suit-case. "You're early for the ferry."

"I know." Her lips twisted to one side. "I thought I'd grab a coffee before I leave. And I'd also intended to call into the station to see you."

"Yeah?"

Feeling suddenly self-conscious, her gaze fell briefly to her shoes. "I wanted to thank you for yesterday."

"Just doing my job," he said with a shrug.

"Yeah," she agreed. "But I think there was more to it than that. Your boss had told you to do nothing. And honestly, I don't think everyone would have believed me." She smiled lightly. "Even *I* thought I might be going crazy at some point, but in the end, you believed me." She shifted her weight, thinking how good it had felt when he'd arrived on the ferry to back her up. "Thank you."

The vulnerability in her words hung between them, and the sudden silence seemed to stretch on.

"Can I join you for that coffee?" he asked eventually.

"Only if you're paying," she said, her words tinged with teasing that changed the atmosphere in an instant.

"I reckon I can stretch to that."

"Were you coming to find me for something specific?" she asked as he took her case for her. Since he had a week off work, she assumed he wasn't coming for an official reason.

"I thought I'd give you a police escort off the island." A dimple puckered his cheek as he smiled. "Make sure we get rid of you."

She snorted a laugh. "Because you're worried about me stealing your job? I reckon I'm the best detective this island has ever seen."

"You might be right." He beamed before his features turned serious. "I do feel a little guilty. You did all the work and I'll get all the credit. Not from my boss, obviously, but I felt like a minor celebrity in the pub last night."

"To be fair, you made the arrest, and I think you did that quite adequately."

"*Quite adequately?*" He slid his gaze to her. "Careful with the compliments. You'll make me blush."

"You don't seem like the blushing type," she said, smiling at him but feeling that heaviness in her chest again. Her time on the Isles of Scilly had gone by far too fast. "You were impressive, though, yesterday. That whole bluffing thing was genius. I don't know how you stayed so calm and confident the whole time."

"There was at least one moment when I didn't dare look at you because I was sure I'd start laughing."

"Me too!" Lily chuckled. "When you said something about a murder investigation and Flora asked if you were serious... all I could think was—"

"*Deadly*," they both said at once, then grinned at each other and burst into laughter.

They were still laughing when Lily's phone buzzed in her pocket. She retrieved it, then shook her head at the screen. "Unknown number. No chance."

PC Grainger gave her a sidelong glance. "I'm surprised. I didn't think you could cope with leaving a mystery unsolved."

She rolled her eyes. "I'm okay with not knowing which company is trying to sell me something today."

They continued in silence for a moment and Lily racked her brain for something to fill it. She enjoyed chatting with Flynn and wanted to take the opportunity to do so while she still could. Apparently, her brain and mouth had lost the connection.

"Sorry you didn't get much of a holiday," he said eventually.

"As weird as it sounds, I actually enjoyed myself."

"Not quite what you planned, though." He gave her one of his playful looks. "Or so I hope."

"No," she said. "Not what I planned at all."

"What *was* your plan?" he asked with a curious twitch of his eyebrow. "Why did you choose Scilly as a holiday destination?"

She slowed her pace as they bypassed the harbour and made for the promenade by Porthcressa Beach.

"I'd been here when I was a kid," she told him, not wanting to get into the details. "I wanted to see what had changed."

"I'll go out on a limb and say *not much*."

"Actually, I think the introduction of the murder mystery holiday is a new concept."

He laughed gently. "I'm not actually sure we should joke about that."

"Police humour, right? It's a coping mechanism."

"Yeah, but you're just a civilian."

"Thanks!"

At the cafe on the promenade, he held the door for her. It seemed to be a popular spot and the window displays showed off beautiful handmade pottery. Inside, shelves displayed more bespoke pottery, and the air was thick with the sweet scent of freshly baked biscuits.

A familiar face smiled at them from a table just inside the door. "Hi," Kit said warmly.

"Hi," Lily replied.

"Feel like joining me?"

When he tipped his head at the chairs beside him, Lily ignored the sinking feeling at the thought that her time alone with PC Grainger was now at an end.

"Thanks." She took a seat while Flynn went to get them coffees. When he returned, it was with a plate of cookies, too.

"You'll have to come back again sometime," Kit said. "Preferably when the weather is better. You didn't get to see much, did you?"

She shook her head. "I didn't see any of the other islands."

PC Grainger dunked a chocolate chip cookie through the foam of his coffee and took a large bite. "It's a strange thing when you're too busy tracking a killer to do any sightseeing."

"It's been a surreal week," she said.

"Do you think you *will* come back?" Kit asked.

"I don't know." Her instinct was to say no. Realistically, she didn't think she'd return. Maybe that was because, in all her travels, she'd rarely returned to the same place once she'd left.

The difference now was that she felt an overwhelming longing to return. It had only been a week, but there was something about this island, and the people she'd met, that made her want to come back.

A loud knock on the window broke her thoughts and had her head snapping up. The scrunched-up face at the glass was familiar, but it took a moment for her brain to catch up and remind her how she knew him. By that time, he was already inside and looming over her.

"I tried calling you." Mr Greaves looked every bit the solicitor with his immaculate suit and a folder resting in the crook of his arm.

"I don't answer if I don't know the number."

"Kind of pointless to give me your number then, really," he huffed, looking slightly out of breath. "Anyway, I need to speak to you about the ice cream shop..."

Chapter Forty-Six

Lily stared up at Mr Greaves while her mind whirred with scenarios of why he suddenly wanted to talk to her about the shop.

"The owner doesn't want to sell," he told her. "But they're happy to lease it to you."

She definitely hadn't been expecting that, and her brain struggled to digest the information.

"What?" Kit asked, stealing the word from the tip of her tongue.

"I don't want to buy it, or lease it." Lily wondered what she'd said to give him that impression. "I was only interested in the history of it. I wanted to know who owned it."

"The owner isn't interested in making new friends, but they are quite keen for you to lease it... with certain stipulations."

"Wait," Kit spluttered. "I'm confused. I've been interested in the business for ages. If they don't want to sell, I'd gladly rent the building."

"It's not available to you," Mr Greaves said dismissively before switching his attention back to Lily. "I can show it to you now," he said, then headed back out of the door without waiting for a response.

Not bothering about her suitcase, Lily jumped to her feet and followed Mr Greaves outside.

"I don't understand," she said, hurrying after him as he strode towards the ice cream shop. "What did you say to the owner to make them think I wanted to rent the place?"

"Nothing. But I'm supposed to keep them informed about anything to do with the shop. If anyone asks about it, I'm supposed to let them know." He stopped in front of the building. Given the peeling paint and the cracked window pane on the front door, Lily was surprised the owners cared enough to want to be kept informed. "After you came to my office, I got in touch with the owner. They didn't have much to say about it until yesterday evening, when I received an email outlining an offer I was to propose to you."

Kit appeared at Lily's side while PC Grainger loomed just behind her.

"What kind of offer?" Kit asked.

"About leasing the shop," Mr Greaves said. "Though I'm not sure why you think it's anything to do with you."

"Didn't you tell them I'm only here for a week?" Lily asked. "I have no interest in leasing a property."

"I can definitely report that back after I've shown you around."

"But I don't need to look around. I'm getting on the ferry in half an hour."

"We should be quick, then." He pulled keys from his pocket and approached the door.

"*I'll* look around," Kit said. "You can tell them *I'll* lease it."

"I'm only authorised to show Miss Larkin the property," he said with a warning glance at Kit.

Mr Greaves held the door for her, but she stayed frozen in place.

"This is weird," PC Grainger said in a tone that made it seem he was talking to himself. "Why would they offer the place to you when it's been closed for so long?"

"It doesn't make any sense at all," she agreed, catching his eye and hoping for some kind of guidance.

His shrug felt encouraging. "I'll wait here," he said. "Shout if there's a problem."

Okay, so now she was even more hesitant to go inside, but she also felt a familiar pang of curiosity and knew she'd always wonder if she didn't find out more.

"Just a quick look," she said, brushing past Mr Greaves as she crossed the threshold.

The room she stepped into was small, with a counter at the back and a stack of stainless-steel tables and chairs at one side. A thick layer of dust covered every surface, and there were dubious-looking stains on the pale blue walls.

"The ice cream making equipment is in the back," Mr Greaves said, and she followed him through to another room, where large metal machines lined the walls. "They're made to last, so the owner is convinced they'll still work."

Lily shook her head, unable to fully register what he was saying while her mind conjured memories of tasting ice cream directly from the machines.

"The rent will be cheap," Mr Greaves was saying. "To compensate for the work you'll need to do to get things up and running again. It's mostly cosmetic. There's also a flat upstairs." He pointed to a flight of stairs at the back corner of the room. "I can show you up there."

"No," she said fiercely, causing him to stop with one foot on the first step. "I don't understand. You need to explain."

"The owner's main stipulation is that the building remains an ice cream shop."

"They want me to restore it and open it again?" she asked, needing all the clarity she could get. "As an ice cream shop?"

"Yes."

"And I could live in the flat upstairs?"

"Yes."

"Why?" She screwed her face up. "Why would they offer that when I didn't ask for it? It's a weird offer to make to a complete stranger."

Mr Greaves nodded his agreement.

"Are they a stranger?" she asked while her chest tightened with trepidation about the answer.

"I'm not at liberty to disclose the identity of the owner," he said.

"If I'm going to lease the shop from them, surely at some point I'll need to at least know their name. And I think I already know it. The owner's name is Gail Greenway, right?"

"I'm not supposed to disclose their name. But that sounds as though you *are* interested in the offer."

"No!" She shook her head vigorously. "I'm interested in knowing who owns the place and why on earth they'd offer to rent it to me."

"If you were to take the offer, you'd need to get used to some secrecy. The owner is a very private person. You'll only ever deal with me."

"But that makes no sense. Why wouldn't they want me to know who they are?"

"I can't say."

"There must be a reason."

"I'm sure there is," he said, retreating from the stairs when it became clear she wasn't going up there.

"I have to go or I'll miss the ferry," she said, annoyed by the whole situation.

"That's a no to the offer then?" he asked, not seeming to care either way.

"Of course it's a no. In which world was it ever going to be anything else? This is the most bizarre thing that's happened to me in a long time. Which is saying something, considering I spent the last week accidentally solving a murder."

"I heard about that," Mr Greaves said with a small twitch of his lips. "Maybe that's why the owners offered you this place. Perhaps they thought you'd be a good addition to the island."

"Don't you even know their reasoning?"

"I only know what I need to know," he said. "Which usually isn't a lot." While he crossed the shop floor, Lily stopped to look around one last time. As her eyes swept the room, they snagged on something on the counter and she moved instinctively towards it.

"What's this?" she asked with a frown.

"What?" Mr Greaves asked with his hand on the door.

"There's an envelope with my name on it." Staring at the swirly writing sent her heart into overdrive.

"I'm no detective," he said. "But I imagine it's a letter for you. Open it and find out."

"Did you put it here?" she asked, head snapping up.

"No. I don't know anything about it."

"Does the owner live on the island? Did they leave me this note?"

"As far as I'm aware, they don't live here." His brow crinkled as though he were also confused. "But nothing would really surprise me at this point." He opened the door and Lily caught the sound of Kit firing questions at him before the door closed behind him.

Hesitantly, she picked up the envelope and slid her finger under the flap.

There was a single sheet of paper inside, folded in half.

Lily's breath caught in her throat as she opened it. The words sent a chill rippling up and down her spine.

I hope you can finally find a home here.

They hadn't signed their name, but had added three kisses.

Lily only tore her gaze from the page when the door eased open again.

"Everything okay?" PC Grainger asked.

Slowly, she shook her head. "It seems I still have a mystery to solve."

Don't miss the next book in the Lily Larkin Mysteries series...

<u>Malicious Intent</u>

Childhood prank, or dark intentions?

After successfully catching a killer, Lily Larkin has gained herself a reputation on the quaint Cornish island of St Mary's.

But her plans to open an ice cream shop mean she doesn't have time for solving mysteries. At least until a teenager turns up on her doorstep claiming he's in danger and begging for her help.

When the boy disappears, he's already given Lily a list of likely suspects.

While the police are convinced it's all a childish prank, Lily isn't so sure. Soon, she's on a mission to find the missing boy and discover the truth behind his disappearance.

Is it a joke gone too far, or is there something sinister at play? Can Lily live up to her reputation and uncover the truth? And when the heat is on, can she solve the case alone or will she find herself enlisting the help of the charismatic local police constable once again?

Also by Hannah Ellis

Fireworks over the Loch (Book 3)

The Cafe at the Loch (Book 4)

Secrets at the Loch (Book 5)

Surprises at the Loch (Book 6)

Finding Hope at the Loch (Book 7)

Fragile Hearts by the Loch (Book 8)

New Arrivals at the Loch (Book 9)

The Lucy Mitchell Series

Beyond the Lens (Book 1)

Beneath These Stars (Book 2)

Always With You (Standalone novel)

The Friends Like These Series

Friends Like These (Book 1)

Christmas with Friends (Book 2)

My Kind of Perfect (Book 3)

A Friend in Need (Book 4)

Hannah has also written a series of children's books aimed at 5-9 year olds under the pen name, Hannah Sparks. The first book is entitled, Where Dragons Fly.

Made in United States
Cleveland, OH
02 March 2026

34024334R00152